Hammer & Tongs:

Conversations in Verse Concerning English Teaching

Michael Skupin

for Joyce Merrill Valdes

Table of Contents

Afternoon

Prof. Malleus accosteth Prof. Forceps

Malleus.   My students writhe and squirm; at times they doze.
Beneath the Spartan mask their boredom shows.
They doodle, sigh and daydream while I sing
Of prepositions, and the joy they bring.
They die a thousand deaths, they say, before   5.
The hour's up; they fidget, sleep some more.
They curse the clock, and hate the class like Hell;
Some file their nails; all strain to hear the bell.
I rant, cajole and brandish charts and books;
They scowl there sullen-faced with martyrs' looks.   10.
Nor clash of rods, projector's blinding ray,
Nor chalkboard true commands them as they stray.
The choicest fruits of yon ditto machine
I spread t'inflame them, still they sit serene.

When old Ulysses to the mast was bound,   15.
At least his ears were teased by Siren sound;
But my disciples, like his wax-eared crew,
Glide off I know not where and dream anew.
While yet my farewell echoes on the breeze,
Their books are gathered, and they clutch their keys. 20.
And lo! the zombie throng that shuffled in
Goes frisking forth to dally, loaf and sin.
I hear a varied babble as they go,
Of heathen tongues; the Bard's they do forego.
Now lordly coaches bear the gang away,   25.
And I bewail another wasted day.
Like Jeremiah now I roam the hall,
Lamenting that I even tried at all.
And yet, as I, distracted, pause to grieve,
I see *your* class, my colleague, will not leave.   30.
Still, still they press with questions, still they yearn
For words and phrases: they are wild to learn.
Behold, Juan leaps and pushes back his chair.
His eyes are wide, his hand is in the air.
Stalwart Mohammed scribbles what you say,   35.
And Helmut goes not answerless away,
Nor Yakov keen will let you go, until
You bless him, and his ears have had their fill.
Like Gideon's squadrons drinking at the shore,

They lay their books not down while heark'ning more: 40.
Their dictionaries proud are yet to hand.
No TOEFL-terrors fright this doughty band.
Reluctantly they part.   They warble clear
The new-discovered tongue they're learning here.
A Delphi-pilgrim, humble I beseech, 45.
Oh, spurn me not, but teach me how to teach!

Forceps.   You rate yourself too low, and me too high.
You want t' improve your skills, and so do I.
Let's take a walk; I'll catch a later bus.
We'll have a drink, and then we can discuss 50.
The status quo of English as a trade:
The breakthroughs, fads and theories that have made
This language-teaching business so involved.
We'll pick through them until your problem's solved.

Malleus.   But soft!   I hear a colleague's charges roar. 55.
It is no riot; he expounds his lore.
Now see, before a rainbow chart he stands.
He opens not his mouth, but waves his hands.
He smites the colors with his wand, as when
Good Moses struck the rock for thirsty men. 60.
Now shrieks and cries of students fill the air.

Their brains are puzzled, and their hearts despair.
The glowering Sphinx now beckons, now doth quell
The moans that from their fevered throats do swell.
In vain they clamor, still he spurs them on,   65.
Breaks silence only when he sees a yawn.
The color-blind, abandoned on the way,
Do pant and squint, but cannot join the fray.
Survivors, though, who master ev'ry hue,
Like Siegfried full of Fafner's blood, construe   70.
Exotic meanings in the world around:
Some see a stripéd sweater, they, a sound.
Whole volumes writ on neckties, socks and skirts,
And mystic runes inscribed on tie-dyed shirts;
The sunset's richness and the bower's shade   75.
Will keep them well-read when their idioms fade.
We leave you, druid, to your language bright,
Beyond our reach, but not beyond our sight.

Forceps.   In vino veritas.   Let's have a beer,
          And talk about the tricks of our career.   80.

In Taberna

Forceps. Before we get specific, let us toast
  Our absent workmates. Aristotle's ghost
  Reminds us not to underestimate
  A student, and Lucretius that a great
  Didactic effort can outlive the man: 85.
  He died; the world reveres his lesson plan.
  Civic Confucius after hours would rush
  To whip out top-notch textbooks with a brush.
  For oral skills our guide is Socrates;
  His self-control can teach us, too. With these   90.
  Examples of our pedigree in mind,
  We pause…remember… privately we find
  A voice, a face, a hand that, years ago –
  How much has happened since! -- took pains to show
  Us monuments of thought, and guide us where   95.
  No one can go without a teacher's care.
  We pay the debt to others, as did they;
  Our helpers now are gone, or far away.

Malleus.   I had an idol like that.   He could teach
  A blockhead how to write or make a speech.   100.

It's now too late to learn his art: he's dead.
But you are here.   Come, tell me what you've read
Or heard that makes your daily lectures thrill,
That makes your students simmer while mine chill,
Assuming that technique is what you've got.   105.
Or were you born a whiz, and I was not?

Forceps.   A prof may be a lemon or an ace,
    But, just as with positions in a race,
    The one in front can slip, the one behind
    Can close the gap, if he makes up his mind.   110.
    Ill health or money woes can make the whiz
    Distracted, and a shell of what he is.
    A novice with self-discipline can fight
    To streamline, amplify, and get it right.
    Now, let me make a bold suggestion here: 115.
    We often get distinctions wrong, I fear.
    Our curse is not dull colleagues, but the gall
    Of wolves with sheepskins who don't teach at all.
    The sexual vulture's one.   I knew a guy
    Who'd ogle female students passing by.   120.

Malleus.   I worked with one the women used to hate.
    He used his craft to help him seek a mate.
    With wit well-armed and bulging bag of tricks,

A new Achilles coming from the Styx!
He offered private lessons to the fair,   125.
Invited Moorish girls into his lair.
Boy will be boys.   But woe betide the lass
Who turned him down after he'd made a pass!
Her body safe, her mind she had to guard:
His lectures frosty grew, he graded hard.   130.
He praised her neighbors, chuckled when she tried
T' express herself, and loudly he denied
That he played fav'rites.   All the students knew
The games he played, despised him, and a few
Complained...

Forceps.   You've made your point.   Enough to say   135.
A teacher doesn't come to school to play.
With private students, nobody should care,
But with a class, it simply isn't fair.
Now brace yourself; here comes my first great rule:
Create an atmosphere of trust.   In school   140.
You see both sheep and goats: complainers loud,
Insistent macho types, and slatterns proud
To show the haggling pow'rs they used back where
They came from.   Don't forget the people there
Are taught to push for all that they can get.   145.
It's nothing personal.   Don't get upset,

But show them all are equal in the room,
For, if you don't, the timid ones won't bloom.
You'll see a transformation of bazaar
Techniques and histrionics that will mar   150.
A classroom's order when they realize
That learning's all that counts, and he who tries
The hardest is the star.   The energy
They've squandered jockeying for place will be
Applied to homework with relentless force.   155.
Make them fanatics and they'll pass the course.
The RX is the same for the wallflow'r:
A massive dose of fairness ev'ry hour.
The shy ones will surprise you, once they know
They won't be bullied.   Then they start to grow.   160.
Encourage them until you're sure, then drive
Them like the other workers in the hive.
Don't let your bright ones coast, or not too much:
A teacher's pet becomes a teacher's crutch.
No resting on past laurels is allowed,   165.
Nor grudges carried day to day.   The crowd
Must start from scratch each hour; trophies they
May win and keep, but only for one day.
Policeman, mother, oracle are you,
Drawing the line, and praising when it's due.   170.
Hope for the best, but keep for ready use

Job's patience and the thunderbolt of Zeus.

Malleus.   Or Jove himself to teach the class.   The task,
As you define it, leaves me out: you ask
For judge, philosopher and umpire, quite   175.
Apart from rhetorician, and you might
As well include a surgeon.   Do you mean
That normal folks don't qualify?   Should green
Beginners quit until they pass the bar
Exam?   Who'll teach the classes, if they are   180.
Reserved for demigods?   What school will teach
Courses that put Olympus in our reach?

Forceps.   That was my first great rule; I have but three.
This was the most important one to me,
And so in point of time I started wrong;   185.
After I've done, you'll see where they belong.
The other two are stepping-stones that make
The first rule second nature.   Let us take
The next one: *Be a student.*   Walk a mile
In shoes your hostages must wear awhile.   190.
Learn what frustration is.   Sit at the feet
Of teachers whose technique is incomplete.
Seek out the ones who ramble.   Thread your way
Through verbal labyrinths.   Observe as they

Meander as they improvise a rule,   195.
Then contradict it later.   Find a school
That teaches you how Tantalus would be
Tormented if the gods should e'er decree
That he be transferred while they drain his pool:
He'd find a vague instructor no less cruel.   200.
But choose some uncouth tongue with script grotesque:
Become Prometheus chained to a desk,
Dependent on your guide, who strolls ahead
And leaves you groping, thirsty and unfed,
Uncaring that you war with symbols strange,   205.
That day by day the rules he gives you change.
You'll realize you'll never close the gap;
The lesson's hard, but you'll avoid the trap
When you begin to teach, because you'll be
Allergic to the symptoms that you see.   210.
Learn what frustration is, to recognize
It when you see it in your students' eyes,
Or face another demon that you must
Encounter, viler than the first, distrust.
Bewilderment will fester when ignored,   215.
For students think the worst when they are bored.
Come, picture if you can the world out there
Beyond the walls of our Valhalla, where
Our colleagues, steady, sober and concerned,

Like diamond-cutters, craftsmen that have learned   220.
To make their job look easy, make you blind
To close encounters with the other kind
That make our pupils skittish.   You have heard,
"The burnt child fears the fire."   Has it occurred
To you that some folks have been burned by those   225.
They've studied under, paying through the nose?
You lamb!   Come, let your mind's eye picture you
A sordid world, ruled by a seedy crew.
A learnéd satyr, madly chasing skirts,
A schoolmarm, when she tries her wings and flirts   230.
Are not contributing to help the team.
Their self-indulgence cancels out esteem
For our profession; nor can we forget
The fly-by-night academies which let
The hucksters that direct them live in style: 235.
Hunger for learning they exploit with guile.
A sleazy room, a dope fiend who can't spell,
Promoted right, support a man right well.
The Hebrews, wand'ring in the wilderness
Their forty years, would feel at home, unless   240.
They knew why from the promised land they're straying:
The less they learn, the longer they keep paying.
No wonder they're suspicious.   Threefold cure
You must effect to remedy the poor

Impressions and bad mem'ries that delay   245.
Their trustingly absorbing what you say:
Concede the past; then show them that it's through,
Proving their verdicts don't apply to you;
Then demonstrate consistently a just
And businesslike behavior they can trust,   250.
And that it's not a fluke, that you intend
To give your best, right to semester's end.
Be thankful for the bitter ones; it's those,
When in your class, that keep you on your toes.
Now, I admit distrust's a special case.   255.
But next, submit to what all students face:
To boredom's tepid cup extend your hand,
And ope your lips to quaff its contents bland.
Aha!   You're shocked to find, like Nordic Thor,
That though you drink and drink, there's always more
     260.

The goblet plain belies a demon's spell:
Once you have drunk, its pow'r begins to tell.
More dread than Lethe wine the devil brew
Goes dribbling on; a subtle poison you
Discern is stealing through your veins, that numbs   265.
Now eye, now ear; now wit itself succumbs.
There's no escaping this enchantment deep:
You cannot leave: your leg has gone to sleep.

Look at your watch.   The second hand does crawl.
The minute hand is moving not at all.   270.
Now sight does fail, replaced by visions hot
Involving winsome classmates, like as not.
The droning's stopped, unless your ears do lie.
You've been called on.   You've no idea why.
Experience boredom so you'll know firsthand   275.
Woe oft inflicted on the student band.
This separates the brown belts from the black,
The conscientious teacher from the hack.
Sample our pharmacopoeia, imbibe
Yourself our nostrums harsh, ere you prescribe.   280.
Frustration, boredom and distrust I show
In homely wise, our fluid status quo:
Pretend they come for wine; don't keep the cup
Just out of reach, but let them drink it up.
If they've been given vinegar instead,   285.
No whiff of it pollute your Bacchus red.
Lastly, don't give them water; but the tart
Elixer that they crave you must impart.
Speaking of which, your glass is empty, sir.
Let us rearm, then take up where we were.   290.

Malleus.   But I'm impatient, eager for your word.
        You have three rules, you say.   Give me the third.

Forceps.　Give me a break to have another round;
　　　　I find terse rules exhausting to expound.
　　　　You do the talking for a while; I'll pause　　　295.
　　　　And let you guess the last one of my laws.

Malleus.　Let's see.　You say each rule's a stepping-stone,
　　　　No maxim standing by itself, alone.
　　　　A student's life's not only drudgery;
　　　　There is a brighter side, we all agree.　　　300.
　　　　Having one's nose rubbed in the nasty part
　　　　Must but perfect a fraction of our art.
　　　　Having refined the ore, the dross we shun,
　　　　But what's the precious substance we have won?
　　　　Wit's alchemy refines th' example's gold　　　305.
　　　　To knowledge gained, to insights manifold.
　　　　I'll take a stab at it: as I discern,
　　　　The last rule is to **Teach them how to learn.**

Forceps.　They'll pick it up from watching you untie
　　　　Knot after Gordian knot as you apply　　　310.
　　　　Lessons you've learned so thoroughly they look
　　　　Like child's play.　They won't learn them from a book,
　　　　But from your habits, mirroring the state
　　　　Of mind that drinks in facts from dawn till late,
　　　　Observing, sifting wheat from chaff, and proud　　　315.

To kneel to Webster with the back unbowed.
You'll find that sober scholarship will keep
Them bustling, if you dare to go in deep;
And if you want to keep them on the floor,
No corny jokes or tales will make them roar   320.
With laughter   as our curious language can:
Its oddities fill out your lesson plan.
Tell them the truth: that "husky" 's soft of voice,
robust, or arctic dog; you take your choice.
Confront your students' goofs, don't let them slide; 325.
You're doing them no favors, and you've lied
If you nod dumbly, filling in the blanks.
Point out their blunders if you want their thanks.
Don't let your Arabs go on eating "bees",
Or tell how "bears" are harvested from trees.   330.
When big brown Spanish eyes are turned on you,
And ask "how many ears" you have, say two.
You doom them all to scorn if you agree
That Venezuelans love to watch TB.
Or if their t.v. sets they "wash" each night,   335.
Save them from future ridicule, set right
Their wayward notions, lovingly but firm,
Like Hamlet, when he made his mother squirm,
But cooler, though uncompromising.   Grant
Them time to grasp the subtleties they can't.   340.

Observe the laws of learning.   You can pose
As Moses only if you've mastered those.
A guide does more than simply read a map.
He needs to have instincts fine-honed on tap
To jump at shortcuts and avoid dead ends;   345.
The group's momentum on his skill depends.
He charts the course to hit oases, towards
Savannahs grassy and the easy fords.
Unerring spot decisions he can make:
His mem'ry tells the fairest route to take.   350.
His caravan arrives without delay,
With unexpected comforts on the way.
Now let me take a slightly diff'rent tack.
Ars est celare artem: there's a knack
To hiding your technique, as Horace taught.   355.
There's twofold satisfaction to be sought
By making class seem casual, off the cuff.
You'll cram more in than if you come on tough;
If you can make relentless drilling seem
To flow without a hitch, you'll build up steam.   360.
A class that has its guard down won't resist
The way they would if you tried to insist
They push themselves.   Slave driver you can be
If you are smooth and they your schemes don't see.
Next there's a private smugness, yours alone.   365.

You see them work their fingers to the bone,
All unsuspecting your intent's to trick
Them into learning, and to make it stick.
Aeneas, when he bore his shield away
From Vulcan's roaring smithy, could not say   370.
What all the hieroglyphics on it meant,
But time revealed th'engraving's high intent.
So let the students, gaily unaware,
Admit the Trojan horse without a care;
Its contents won't emerge until you've gone.   375.
They'll only grasp your deftness later on.
Concoct a wassail sweet, but spike it strong.
You'll see th' ingredients' effect ere long.
To pull it off, though, keep a poker face:
Of secret motives show them not a trace.   380.
Be brisk and businesslike.   When things go right,
You cool demeanor kindles warmth and light.
Your job's to teach and give them time to learn.
You are the flint, they are the ones who burn.

Malleus.   You make it sound so simple.   Let me rest;   385.
Your insights will take some time to digest.
These cryptic slogans commentary need,
But, ouch!   They do hit close to home indeed

Forceps.   Sleep on them, then.   My friend, it's getting late.

Malleus.   To save my ego while I ruminate,   390.
    I'll walk you to the bus stop, if I may,
    And ask specific questions on the way.

Forceps.   I wish you would.   I want to know if I
    Have given counsel that will not apply.
    King Solomon once said: correct a fool   395.
    And he will hate you; it's the wise man who'll
    Be grateful if you catch him off the track.
    Lay on, Macduff, and pull no punches back.

Malleus.   What happens when fanatics plague a class?
    Picture a group divided by the crass   400.
    Extremes of Koran-thumping sexists loud
    In league with condescending machos proud,
    Determined not to let a chance go by
    To ridicule the women as they try
    To ask a question or to answer one;   485.
    And on the other hand, let's say that none
    Among the females make it easy to
    Feel much respect for what they say and do:
    For some of them are cowed and insecure;
    One is a disco queen; one blindly pure;   490.

One shows some promise, but can only harp
On worn-out Marxist strings with insults sharp.
And there you are, with squabbling in the air.
What can you do, assuming that you dare?

Forceps.   My instincts say, when tension's running high,   415.
To take Job's wife's advice: lie down and die.

Malleus.   I think you have a better answer.   Let
Me tell about another trial you get.
Assume a different class, a decent lot,
But cursed with one fanatic on the spot: 420.
A sniper who takes ev'ry chance to praise
Some crazy tyrant for his loony ways
And wish out loud that you would find the truth
And   rev'rence for his fetishes uncouth.
He slouches, shoulders hunched and vision bleared,   425.
Always exactly three days' growth of beard;
As Hercules would wear a lion hide,
A faded Army jacket is his pride,
Though fashions change: it's only been a while
Since plain brown groc'ry bags were still in style,   430.
Worn on the head to muffle chants they'd utter,
These Dapper Dans who'd set girls' hearts aflutter.
But there he sits, his paper bonnet doffed.

You've asked someone a question; he has coughed
Politely; clearer omen never came.   435.
He'll interrupt and try to play his game.
The other students didn't come to hear
His drivel, or to see his cocksure sneer.
The moment calls for action.

Forceps.   No, it calls
For preparation.   Listen, comrade, all's   440.
Decided in the first few days.   You crack
The whip and come on strong, but show no lack
Of patience for the man beneath the mask.
It's worth the trouble.   Healing's not your task,
But you must give the guy a chance to shed   445.
Taboos and shibboleths and lies he's read.
But draw the line.   Permit no butting in,
Nor let him endless, aimless stories spin.
The savage that annoys you's the result
Of revolution, war, corruption, cult.   450.
Restrain the monster, but the soul respect,
Not hoping for immediate effect.
The answer's siege, not skirmish: quell the clown
The way a trick'ling stream wears granite down.

Malleus.   I'll ask another question as we wend   455.
   Our busward way.   Why is it that you tend
   To dress more dashingly than others do?
   You wear a tie; no scuff does mar your shoe;
   Your socks do match; you button up your shirt;
   No reeking perfumes cause the sinus hurt.   460.
   Do you expect the others to conform?
   Do you believe they'll leave the uniform
   Of cut-offs, t-shirts, sneakers and the fair
   Aspect of sunglasses perched in their hair?
   Is this one-upmanship to make the rest   465.
   Of us look bad compared with how you're dressed?

Forceps.   To each his own.   My wardrobe fits my style.
   One could teach English wearing but a smile.
   I try to meet the students halfway, though.
   Their expectations dictate that I show   470.
   No nonsense in the way I come across.
   I drive them hard; my tie makes me the boss.

Malleus.   I've heard you never gesture to enhance
   Your explanations.   If you had the chance,
   Wouldn't you like to fill the gap?   Explain   475.
   Why one can't teach and also entertain.

Forceps. I used to gesture wildly, till the time
    I took a summer off and studied mime.
    Oh yes, I did.   The flailing stopped for good.
    If I were stricken mute, of course I could   480.
    Get "bicycle" and "rope" across and "walk
    Against the wind" without a lot of talk,
    But knowledge of the art will cool its charms.
    The more you know, the less you wave your arms.
    There's built-in condescension in the choice   485.
    Of hands and eyes instead of ears and voice.
    Stick to the high road: use your wit to pick
    The words that let your pupils catch on quick.
    The words are there; the students are not dumb.
    So fold your arms, let inspiration come,   490.
    But on a flatt'ring level.   Make it clear
    You trust them to decipher what they hear.
    Don't panic if they sit there like a stone;
    Try something else, but keep an adult tone.

Malleus.   Which, by extension, also would leave out
    Teaching them songs in grammar's place, no doubt.

Forceps.   I disagree.   You take my point too far.
    Music's not kid stuff.   Take up your guitar
    And churn away.   Consider what you gain:

You're teaching words and diction, and you train   500.
Them in the rhythms of the English tongue,
For sounds are best remembered when they're sung.
On top of that, you help them break the ice
When they meet gringos, so you're helping twice.

Malleus.   Just when I think that things are going well,   505.
   My class comes in disgruntled, nor will tell
   The cause until I press them, though I know.
   In lab assignments I've a ways to go.
   Like John on Patmos, words do not convey
   What's going on inside as I survey   510.
   The panoply of gadgets that await
   My word, ere dealing out my students' fate.
   I quail before the television screen;
   The board could pilot any submarine;
   Cassettes in serried ranks at me do frown.   515.
   I thumb the catalog, then put it down.
   This fancy gear is mine, to do my will,
   But bumbling I began and bumble still.
   Tom Edison and other clever men
   Have given me the chance, time and again   520.
   To be a Daedalus or Phaeton…

Forceps.   That's Icarus, though both flew at the sun,
    And both misused their power and did harm.
    The symptoms were the same: they both got warm,
    A sign that trouble wasn't far away.   525.
    They shrugged it off, and where are they today?
    If your disciples discontented plod
    Through tape lab portals, if they start to nod
    Within that citadel, you've warning clear.

Malleus.   Now, wait a minute.   Much as I revere   530.
    Your learning, Phaeton did fly the star
    Itself, not to it…

Forceps.   As the fables are
    They both do fit.   The teacher loses face,
    The students suffer torments in the place.
    Before th' infection gets a chance to spread   535.
    And keep your suff'ring students home in bed,
    Quick diagnose the source of phlegm, and spare
    Your ego not, but find what's wrong in there.
    Do uninspiring   drills them drowsy make?
    Then make your own.   Your self-respect's at stake. 540.
    Do silly tales insult their intellect?
    Get hot ones to make up for your neglect.
    Refer to line one hundred eighty-nine,

And purge the lab of influences malign.
If empathy for students is your guide,   545.
They'll queue up, clamoring to get inside.
The lab director and his cherubim
Must be your allies, so consult with him:
His myrmidons must execute the plan;
His expertise can benefit your clan.   550.
Quick, cast your eyes aloft!   An omen's there!
You see an eagle cleave serene the air;
Now suddenly twelve swans assail him hard.
Watch close; unless I am a faulty bard,
We'll see an illustration in the sky.   555.
The swans do nip and wheel, yet stay not nigh.
The eagle lower glides, but strikes not back;
They sense he will not fight against the pack,
And draw off in surprise, then let him be.

Malleus.   The omen I accept.   The eagle's me.   560.
My yamm'ring students are the swans.   I must
Accept their grievances without a fight, on trust,
T' encourage them to speak their minds.   Then I
Must act, if they are right; if not, then try
T' avoid resentment at their whimpers vain;   565.
They know not what they do.   The wrath will wane.
Speaking of omens, yesternight I dreamed

A vision strange, nor know I what it seemed.
A sheltered garden, plashing waters' sound
And music sweet involved my students round.   570.
They sat enthroned in fatly cushioned chairs;
Their eyes were closed, their minds were free from cares;
The room was dark; the guru's velvet croon
Emerged from somewhere, causing me to swoon.
His lecture was like muzak, smooth but cool: 575.
Sweet nothings did he murmur to his school.
A dream within a dream did then occur:
A blizzard howled, I knew not where we were.
The teacher, decked in fur, stood forth, I say,
And on a three-stringed triangle did play.   580.
I woke up sweating, vaguely ill at ease.
Can augury unfold such dreams as these?

Forceps.   From fair Siberia's meadows comes this tack.
McDonald's thought of it a few years back,
But couldn't quite depers'nalize it pure.   585.
The surly Slavs, though, caught by its allure
Refined it till it mirrors their sad role:
Somnambulistic, easy to control,
Foolproof by definition: recipe
And formula are all, it seems to me.   590.
They lounge there passive, soaking up the sounds,

Then out it comes.   Their glibness knows no bounds.
Mark well, if you would wreathe your brows with bays,
Import your fancies and you'll garner praise.
No home-grown theory ever will compete   595.
Unless barbarian relics are its seat
And cornerstone; an Ethiopic chart
Can be enhanced to decorate your art,
If stripped of context and with notions new
Puffed up, unless your bluff is called.   Review   600.
The way the Volga gangsters train their spies;
The Jonestown education system wise;
The way the Mongols taught their steeds to rear;
How Srivijaya shamans made things clear;
In deadly earnest dissect subtleties   605.
Of how head-hunters share their gory keys
To mast'ry of their piquant art.   Declare
That gold is where *you* find it: anywhere.
Then, in exotic rags and tatters dressed,
Proclaim your emperor's new clothes the best.   610.
Look everywhere but in the mirror for
The reason class is often such a bore.
Behind the petticoat of System hide,
So when your class complains they can't abide
The status quo, and that you have to get   615.
your act together, lash out!   Nor abet

Constructive criticism: glare at them,
Your knuckles white from clutching fast the hem
Of Method's robe, or, if you will, the horn
Of System's altar; face them down with scorn,   620.
And sanctimonious invoke arcane
Excuses for your classroom ways inane.
Nirvana-like, you find yourself exempt
From student input, shielded by contempt
For all save System buzzing in your ear.   625.
Take up your bed and walk!   Cast down your dear
Addicting crutches; confident embark
Upon the real adventure.   Leave the Ark
And start your Odyssey.   Leave on the shelf
Your pretty bibles; chart your course yourself.   630.
Karate masters aren't supposed to need
To wear a pistol on each hip.   To feed
His customers a chef needs not to ask
For frozen t.v. dinners for the task.
They both need tools: *gi* 's stoves are absolutes.   635.
I don't complain of tools, but substitutes
For polish and attention giv'n by you
To student needs, and to their talents, too.
Allow yourself only a peasant pride.
Pose not as theoretician rarefied.   640.
Confuse not fish stories with fishing: you're

Kidding yourself until your drop your lure.
'Tis writ that Mithradates King did prate
In thirty languages; in pomp he sate
And rattled off his orders to the thralls   645.
Who bore his mandates from the palace halls
Throughout his polyglot dominions sans
Interpreter to mistranslate his plans.
The Phrygian tongue upon his tongue did trip;
The Lydian did vault his nether lip;   650.
His nasals rivaled bumblebees in flight;
His Hittite glottal stops came out just right.
When embassies from vasty Ind did call,
Or Cathay's saffron sons approached the wall,
He'd waft exotic greetings as they'd kneel,   655.
Then listen to them till he got the feel
Of what their gibberish was all about.
In no time flat he had it figured out,
And babbled with them pleasantly, received
Their messages and sent them home relieved.   660.
No grunting slaves did turn his reel-to-reel
Recorder, and unless his spies would steal
Those kiln-dried monoliths with notches knicked
From other royal libraries, he picked
Up foreign languages without the aid   665.
Of books we now think vital to our trade.

He knew the process, centuries before
Our modern thinkers codified their store
Of tactics, strategies, approaches, styles.
The process antedates the subtle wiles   670.
Of standardizers since.   A Czech cliché
Asserts some truth in everything   you say;
The theoretic Babel hold to light;
You find an alloy of the false and trite,
With dainty nuggets bedded in the slag.   675.
Where is the mother lode whence comes the swag?
The truth is in the trenches.   There we learn.
Though Sinai's slopes we scan, no bushes burn.
The lights we see are lanterns of a throng
Of treasure hunters spending vigils long.   680.
They overturn each stone, and midnight oil
Is sacrificed t' illuminate their toil.
So, wish them luck, and glance from time to time
In their direction as they barefoot climb
From crag to holy crag.   Remember, though,   685.
Nihil novum sub solem: there is no
New thing under the sun, the Preacher's view.
Be ready for exceptions, but for few.
In any case, Mosaic laws would fail:
Our art is a mosaic of detail.   690.
Each tile is polished sep'rately, and fit

Delib'rately, the pattern bit by bit
Expanding as you find a way to make
Each grammar point more vivid, and to wake
Semantic consciousness and sense of style.   695.
To do it, keep a thousand tricks on file,
Specific remedies for language ills,
The way a modern doctor gives out pills.
Medieval doctors held on to their jobs
By using mumbo-jumbo with the mobs.   700.
Specific problems didn't bother them.
When faced with plague, they'd blandly talk of phlegm,
Or balance of the sanguine with the bile.
They'd memorized abstractions infantile,
The passwords of their idle guild, that veiled   705.
The reasons that their voodoo always failed.
Despite the jargon grand and logic tight,
The bottom line was always "Bleed 'em white."
A pox on those who solemnly revive
Elitist pseudoscientific jive!   710.
Once, for a joke, a friend appointed me
The "Academic Flexibility
Options Coordinator" for a day.
(I've never used it on a resume.)
Alarmed, I see our boyish prank reborn   715.
As longer titles desks and doors adorn.

The pidgin spreads.   Not only heraldry,
But journals murky grow with its debris.
More light!   Fresh air!   Such vampire habits shun!
We've naught to hide.   We flourish in the sun.   720.
The best vocabulary text I know
Is found between the lines in *Euthyphro*.
Classroom dynamics?"   Much was said indeed
In *Mother*, where Brecht's workers learn to read.
If you must venture into shadow-land,   725.
At least seek out a guide who's truly grand.
But note where Dante's Socrates does dwell:
In limbo.   (Brecht, of course, would be in Hell.)
There's wisdom there.   In limbo let them be.
Experience is your lamp and only key.   730.
No matter how sublime your mentors loom,
You've far to go, so leave them in the tomb.
Your eyes, your ears, your brain guide you alone
To Ithaca, along a path unknown.
From Boreas' corner manna comes my way: 735.
I see my bus, the last one of the day.
Now break we off, although we've but begun.
We'll meet again mañana for more fun.

Malleus.   But tarry still! I've questions more to pose.

Forceps.   Well, answer them yourself.   The chap who knows
                                                                                    740.
The answers is no hero; what takes thought
Is coming up with questions.

Malleus.   Here I ought
To tell you that the questions aren't mine,
At least the best ones.   I could not refine
And focus on my woes, so went around   745.
And asked my able colleagues what they'd found.
Their smiles told me they knew the answers, yet
They spoke in riddles that I didn't get.

Forceps.   They knew you had a brain, and gave you clues.
Pick up the gauntlet, take it home and muse.   750.
So long.

Malleus.   A minute more!

Forceps.   No, thar she blows.

Malleus.   One other thing…

Forceps.   Oh, please!

Malleus.   Before we close,
      Just let me say...   He's gone.   I wanted pat
      Solutions to my faults.   He left me flat.
      He's forcing me to take his heavy hint: 755.
      Instead of gobbling everything in print,
      He bids me thrive on puzzles.   Be it so.
      My class won't tolerate the status quo,
      So I'll turn inward and evaluate
      My good points and the things my students hate.   760.
      Less smoke, more fire my motto be from hence,
      The flame besmothered not with papers dense,
      But blazing bright, whipped up by common sense.

Envoy

You'd criticize a lim'rick if it took
Analysis to make its meaning clear.   765.
I spent long hours on Rilke's sonnet-book;
I didn't understand it for a year.

The book you hold is neither deep nor terse:
The theme's too broad for me to boil down
To five keen lines of deathless, vivid verse;   770.
A clown in epic robes is still a clown.

Will Shakespeare's fools are entertaining guys,
Ambiguous in speech and long on nerve.
They risk the rod to make their hearers wise;
They show their love by needling those they serve. 775.
I've teased a bit, but borne ill will toward none.
Farewell!   My homely teaching-poem's done.

❋ Hammer & Tongs

Morning

When last I wrote, I said that I was through;
I give myself the lie by writing more.
I left loose ends in what I wrote before,
But not all that you read will be review.
Right heartily I start my second chore;   5.
A new word-puzzle's challenge tempts me, too,
As well as thoughts inspired by the crew
I work with, who have looked the first part o'er.

Be patient with my solo quilting-bee.
The product is for you, a comforter   10.
Where beauty's second to utility.
No ill-stitched purple patches will occur.
Accept this home-made, hand-made gift from me,
And tell me quick when you find that I err.

Prof. Malleus telephoneth Prof. Forceps.

I paced the floor, then tossed and turned last night.   15.
    Ideas kept boiling up; the things you said
    Kept teasing after I'd switched off the light.

At last the sandman came, but in my head
    Our talk went on, expressed in symbols strange:
    Queen Mab came gliding up; Nepenthe fled.   20.

I woke, methought, deep in a mountain range,
    With crags about and boulders heaped around;
    Low sulking clouds that made the shadows change

Sailed sullen overhead; there was no sound
    Of bird or bug from scrubby pines that stood   25.
    Aslant, more roots atop than underground.

I squinted; something stirred in that grim wood.
    There!   Left!   Darting from tree to tree a slender
    Phantom prowled as no mortal hunter could.

A Japanese I saw in three-piece splendor.   30.
   'Twas no mistake: the guy was stalking me.
   He cupped his hands, called on me to surrender

My teaching post to someone who might be
   Up to the job.   "Depart, or else!" his cry.
   That hit a nerve.   I couldn't disagree.   35.

Then, on the right a scurry caught my eye;
   An Arab clad in earth-tones scrambled o'er
   The boulders there, zigzagging, drawing nigh.

The welkin rang, echoing to his roar:
   "There is no god but God, but as for you   40.
   There must be someone else less of a bore."

I trembled there, transfixed with fear and rue.
   "Hey, guys," I stammered, "from now on, you'll see,
   Things will be diff'rent."   Still they nearer drew.

I rose, unsure whether to stand or flee   45.
   Then horror-stricken I began to run,
   On seeing apparition number three:

With sooty lashes, lipstick like the sun
 A lanky Latin venus reared and pawed
 The air, her bracelets clanking one on one.   50.

There was no time to marvel or be awed.
 Behung with ghastly trophies was her breast,
 Betokening in gold: Beware the Broad!

I fled the threesome, pausing not to rest.
 But fleeter they; enclosed on every side   55.
 I strove amain to scape their vengeance-quest,

But jagged rocks were messing up my stride.
 I fell down in a heap, resolved to try
 My lifelong gen'ral purpose rule: to hide.

I cast about; I saw a cave nearby,   60.
 So staggered in. But hark! Footfall! And lo,
 A lantern carried by some other guy

From deep within the cavern. By its glow
 I saw a toga'd gent with laureled brow
 Come sidling up with gouty gait and slow.   65.

"I get it! Mantuan! Prince of Poets! Wow!
Arms and the man! Now, get me out of here."
"Vergil's retired," he said; "I'm tour-guide now.

"I'm Horace; you recall – Latin, fifth year.
A real glutton for punishment were you.
I'm doing you a favor, let's be clear: 70.

"On paper I'm semi-retired, but knew
You liked my *Odes*, so gave a fan a break.
Lord knows, these days the Latinists are few.

"Yourself, you lack the horsepower to make   75.
It through my *Satires*, which is just as well.
New tongues must have their turn. Let's take

"A little tour through diff'rent parts of Hell
That you'd find interesting, the ones that touch
Your trade, where fallen English teachers dwell.   80.

The torments they endure, you see, are such
As mirror... Hey, what's wrong? Give me a clue."
"I just thought Vergil... No, it's nothing much."

"He read part one, and figured I would do.

    Chin up.   I know my way around, you'll see.   85.

    What's good for Pope is good enough for you."

He beckoned, strolled away; I sheepishly

    Came tagging after.   "Master," quoth I, "whence

    The wails mixed in with demon's cackling glee?"

"We're at Hell's threshold.   Here's where we commence; 90.

    We'll see the seamy side of Karma-land,

    But just a tiny nook of this immense

"Establishment.   Please note that it was planned,

    Designed and built by students who'd been stung

    By profs whose brows now bear Lord Belial's brand

                                      95.

"(Alias Moloch, in whose mouth were flung

    Young victims; call him Mammon, or invoke

    Astarte foxy – use names Milton sung).

"Alive they strutted; here they bear the yoke

    Of torments tailor-made to fit their sins;   100.

    Fit punishment awaits them when they croak.

"You see that gate?   That's where our trek begins.
    Mark well the doom across the cornice graved
    And then the fate of Sloth's dead paladins."

"UNCOUTH WE CAME, AND NAUGHT BUT LEARNING CRAVED:
                                                                        105.
WE ASKED FOR LOAVES, YOU GAVE US STONES
INSTEAD.
NOW WALK THE ROAD YOR SELF-INDULGENCE
PAVED.

"YOU'LL FIND A NOVEL LOOKING-GLASS AHEAD.
YOU WON'T GO THROUGH IT, 'CAUSE YOU'RE
STUCK HERE, FRIEND.
NOW, TAKE YOUR MEDICINE," the motto read.   111.

I scanned it twice, but didn't comprehend.
    "Explain he riddle," I implored my Chief.
    I must needs grasp it ere we more descend."

He shook his head, disgusted.   "That, in brief,
    Is why you may wind up here when you die,   115.
    And that's why you've already come to grief.

"If you can't read with analytic eye,
    Unaided by explanatory notes,
    Your students will begin to wonder why

"You blindly go on ramming down their throats   120.
    A double standard, mother of all wrong:
    They feast on challenges; you swallow quotes.

"Pay close attention as we move along.
    We've reached th' infernal bailey where are mewed
    A fiend-scourged crew: the *Monolingual* throng."

I then descried a cap'ring goblin brood
    A-flogging miscreants whose groans were muffled
    By tongues of fire-hose size that did protrude

Between their lips and dragged the ground: they shuffled,
    Harried by flailing scourge, but burdened sore.   130.
    I turned and shrugged to Horace; quite unruffled,

He cleared his throat and spoke: "Forevermore
    The dullest bunch that e'er rode Charon's barge
    Must pay the bill they walked on t'other shore.

"Now, here's a double standard: while at large   135.
    They posed as owls, remaining language-callow,
    Flightless, instructing nestlings in their charge

"Uncurious in life, their mouths lay fallow;
    They'd read that sans another tongue's perspective
    Your knowledge of your own must needs be shallow,   140.

"But shrugged the proverb off, and stayed defective,
    Their ignorance proclaiming ev'ry day:
    'I'll help you reach your linguistic objective.

'My methods don't help me in any way,
    But trust me, you – I can't pronounce your name;   145.
    I'm too afraid of being laughed at.   May

'I probe your secrets in a classroom game?
    (Don't ask me mine.   That's very rude of you.)
    Where in the hell's the land from which you came?

'Do as I say, ignoring what I do.   150.
    My methods are much better than you'd guess
    If facts influenced inf'rences you drew

'From my own less than thundering success
    With languages.   You must have faith in me,
    In spite of my linguistic helplessness.'   155.

"Let's leave this den of language atrophy
    And move along to check exhibit two
    Where misdeeds boomerang to misery."

We trudged along, with no torments in view,
    Just gloaming near and void beyond.   My nose,   160.
    However, caught a scent that stung, and grew

Viler; as when the tangy wind that blows
    From dump to bower makes the guests curtail
    Their party chat, and brisk flirtation slows,

So sagged my mood as we went down the trail: 165.
    The stench transformed my smugness into dread.
    I held my nose to guard the sinus frail,

And wiped the tears my smarting eyén shed.
    I dimly saw my Leader stay and wheeze.
    "The fen where skulk the *Condescending* dead   170.

"Whose manners smothered students' energies
   By treating them like children, now you smell.
   They're pent for aye in gargoyle nurseries,

"Their diapers never changed, as you can tell.
   They've teething rings and rattles t'exercise   175.
   Their minds and tongues, a backwards parallel

"To hours spent having Arabs analyze
   Th' Arabian Nights rehashed or Germans ken
   Grimm's Fairy Tales diluted, in the guise

"Of 'learning as a child learns.'   Boys once men   180.
   And girls, not women, bit the bullet while
   Dear Teach went over Mother Goose again,

"Stymied by gush, laid low by masklike smile.
   Promiscuous parenthood is hard to fight,
   But, though ridiculous, is nothing vile;   185.

"So here in Hell we own a diff'rence slight:
   Light tortures for the ones entrapped on Earth
   By blind emotion; greater torments light

"On those who tied their students' hands by dearth
    Of information.   Spoon-fed they remained   190.
    Tongue-tied and docile, targets for the mirth

"Of yonder tyrants, scolded when they strained
    To set their keepers' right: their hints were taken
    As mutiny, and met with tantrums feigned.

"Pity the student!   From adult to shaken   195.
    Beginner with an ego made of glass!
    Recall the odyssey they've undertaken,

"And minimize your little iliads crass.
    We'll mosey on and let this congregation
    Luxuriate in what they brought to class."   200.

I pensive waxed as we detoured the station,
    And asked wry Horace, "Poet, say, will we
    Behold my foredoomed hellish recreation?"

He frowned.   "Well, speaking hypothetic'lly,
    You'd throw them for a loop if ere you woke   205.
    You came to join the great Majority."

"Oh, hypothetic'lly, of course.   I'll go for broke
    Once I get out of here, and I'll fly straight.
    But why the puzzlement?   Is this a joke?"

"Oh, no.   Now I can only speculate,   210.
    But placing you with your offending kin
    Might stump them, as your record indicate."

"I guess they'd have to spread me pretty thin,
    Or shuttle me around from doom to doom.
    It might be too much work to put me in."   215.

"Don't worry.   They've been warned that, since the boom
    In English teaching, they'll have lots to do.
    They've hired extra help; they'd find you room.

"But why the fatalism?   What you view
    Should put some starch in your career above.   220.
    You've seen what slacking off up there leads to;

"You came a crow; return as Noah's dove.
    Straight don the mystic emblem of   your art:
    Brass knuckles underneath a velvet glove.

"We're hard upon Hell's next instructive part.   225.
    Hear you the music?   Smell the popcorn stale?
    Our meetings with the *Socialites* now start."

'Neath   streamers, lit with Japan lanterns pale,
    Card tables by the thousand stretched before
    My sight, and dated songs did ear assail.   230.

Around each board were huddled five or more
    Unsmiling ones who gloomy gazed upon
    Wee winking candles.   Burning to explore

This not-quite Mardi Gras, I'd nearer drawn.
    Then I was noticed.   Night and day!   They greeted   235.
    Me raucously as guinea hens at dawn.

The horde with waving arms and howl entreated
    My company, yet mobbed me not withal:
    They strained and clutched and clamored, but stayed seated.

My sleeve was grabbed, and chairward did I fall.   240.
    E'en ere I lit mine hosts did rend the air
    With shoptalk, each trying to louder squall.

I broke away, was flung t' another chair.
    This group reeled off credentials, screeching wild.
    Again I fled, was captured, had to bear   245.

Convention anecdotes this time, again exiled
    Myself by force – in vain! -- only to be
    Held hostage elsewhere; my new captors smiled

And bawled of former programs, and the fee
    They got.   At last I saw a table close   250.
    Where all the chairs save one were teacher-free.

I toward it lunged, and kicked away the gross
    And clawing fingers at my trouser leg.
    "Don't say a word," I hissed.   "*You* get the dose,

"Not me.   I'm not dead yet, so stuff it.   Now, I beg   255.
    Your pardon, sir, for being blunt.   Let's chat."
    "You spoke aright to take me down a peg

"Before I started babbling ere you sat.
    Your words have lifted for a time my spell.
    We're never heard here, see?   We're just talked at." 260.

"But why," asked I, "the shrieking?"   "Can't you tell?
    We shunned the truest source of teachers' kicks:
    The joy of seeing minds and tongues grow well,

"Developing, helped by our teaching-tricks:
    From lisping language crawl to walk, then run.   265.
    We cheated them.   Here they get in their licks.

"Circe's successors we, we gave them fun:
    We spared the trellis, and they went to seed.
    Approval-starved, enforcing standards none,

"We lulled, then numbed them with our mellow creed.   270.
    Handshakes and hugs and ill-pronounced good-byes
    At term's end met our pedagogic need.

"Why are we here?   Too late the class got wise.
    Rebuffed by registrars' sarcastic smirk,
    And shipwrecked by entrance tests, they'd despise   275.

The giddy hours when lovingly we'd shirk
    The nuts and bolts of English, concentrating
    On sharing, caring, sparing them the work

"Of strengthening their skills.   Exasperating
　　Collegiate Waterloos would make them wish   280.
　　We'd partied less and done more explicating.

"Eheu, fugaces!   wrote your Guide.   We'd dish
　　Out cotton candy.   Posthumous, the years
　　Drag bitter by for our ways Neroish.

"Just as our parties bored students to tears   285.
　　We sit here bored.   Just as it never dawned
　　On us that what was music to our ears

"And fun for us might leave them cold, we've yawned
　　For decades now.   About ten years ago
　　I realized how party hounds who fawned   290.

"And flattered kept my teaching level low:
　　They fed the fire.   But that's not the whole story:
　　As they in life, we aren't free to go.

"My parties weren't exactly mandatory,
　　But those who came became a deadly clique;   290.
　　The others, outcasts; my class, purgatory,

"Where trusties ruled the teacher's bailiwick."
    "Eheu fugaces," I echoed.   "Well, I'll
    Pass on your tale.   I hope it does the trick."

I glanced about, then sprinted for the aisle.   300.
    The tables skirted safe, I peered to find
    Where Horace had been loitering the while.

I spied him with another of his kind;
    I cautious neared and heard them arguing.
    They paused and turned as I stole up behind.   305.

My Bard spoke first.   "This fellow's name should ring
    A bell: it's Cato, who, I must point out,
    Has no position here, but came to bring

"An invitation to a tour about
    His territory."   "Let me speak," began   310.
    The other.   "Though my tendency to shout

"Down decadence has branded me, I can
    Point to a higher credit, less well-known,
    Inspiring, I daresay, to any man:

"Well past the age when most grown-ups have grown   315.
    Complacent, I resolved to start from scratch
    And make the Greeklings' sparkling tongue my own.

"Old dog, new tricks, you know.   I found the catch
    Was fear of being laughed at: the frustration
    Would paralyze me.   Habits that attach   320.

"Themselves to civic pow'r and social station
    Ill suit the requisite humility
    For aping foreigners' pronunciation.

"But swallowing patrician vanity
    I did quite well until I died.   Down here   325.
    I run a place I'm sure you'll want to see,

"A parallel Inferno, meant to cheer
    Discouraged pedagogues above; 'twas built
    To fill the hearts of rascal kids with fear.

"In Students' Hell they expiate their guilt.   330.
    You'll see them all: the Ape-Man, Sloth, Buffoon,
    Dumb Broad, Playboy – they get it to the hilt."

"Perhaps some other dream," I answered.   "Soon
    The dawn will rouse my slumb'ring members, and
    My first task is to break from my cocoon.   335.

"I'll tell my colleagues, though, that there's a land
    Where classroom hoboes get their just deserts.
    I'll take a rain check.   Hope you understand."

"Oh, sure," replied the Censor.   "What averts
    Your destiny from here must take first place;   340.
    You're on the right track if you wince: truth hurts."

A pair again, the Puglian set the pace.
    We briskly stepped.   I sensed that time was short.
    I saw a look of loathing on his face.

"The things we've seen are of a trifling sort   345.
    Compared with what's ahead."   "Trifling!" I cried.
    "You mean that wasted time's of no import?

"That foisting self-indulgence, justified
    By rationalizations glib, on those
    Who trusting came, but found their patience tried,
                                 350.

"Good will abused…"   "You think the culprits chose
    To let dark corners of the mind and heart
    Dictate their lives?   Borrowing Cicero's

"Approach, don't think of them as not too smart
    Or consciously malignant, for their flaws   355.
    Stemmed from their blind spots, blemishing their art.

"Reread your Emerson, and trust the laws
    Of compensation to chastise in just
    Degree.   You'll see the diff'rence when we pause

"Down there – you see the thicket and the dust   360.
    Clouds?   Penny-ante stuff we leave astern.
    Henceforth we're dealing with the upper crust

"Of teaching sinners, but I'll let you learn
    Yourself the line that separates the small
    Fry from the sharks."   "Avast!"   I said.   "I burn

"With sudden inspiration!   What you call
    Minor offenders limited their scope
    They fooled around a bit, but that was all.

"Bear with me, for I've further yet to grope;
    Let's see.   The crimes get worse.   Worse than abuse
                                             370.

    Of learning's laws?   But students often cope

"And learn in spite of teachers' habits loose.
    Wait!   Blame the waiter if the food is cold,
    But if it's bad, the chef's head's in the noose."   375.

"You're getting warm.   The bushes yonder hold
    Entrapped the *Pidginmongers* who'd pollute
    The tongue itself.   They took disciples' gold,

"Told them gringos would think their accents cute
    And barbarisms clear.   Pure sabotage!
    They axed all hope of progress at the root."   380.

"Then those within, despite their camouflage
    Are mirror images of those before:
    There truth badly presented's the menage;

"Here slickness reigns and English counts no more
    My Poet smiled.   "We've crossed the halfway line.
                                             385.

    The things we've seen will tell you what's in store."

Now single file, hemmed in by tangled vine
　　Aloft and tripped by undergrowth below,
　　I groped after my Leader's lantern-shine.

He slowed, then turned; he'd found something to show.　390.
　　I gasped.　I recognized the Hell-pent scamp.
　　It gives you pause to see someone you know

Down there, however logical.　The lamp
　　Revealed a form trapped a la Absalom,
　　But pinioned worse: a vegetable clamp　　395.

Gripped arms and legs as well.　My former chum
　　Wide-eyed began with "Who-ee debbil you?"
　　Then, "You no speakee," as I stood there dumb,

"Dam-me, I killee!"　"That's the guy I knew.
　　You haven't changed a bit, but won't you drop　400.
　　The baby talk?"　He sighed, "Me no can do.

"Big persons here, they no let persons stop
　　From speak like when I teach before two jeers
　　In my country."　"Well, I sincerely hop

"That not is permanent," fighting back tears   405.
    I said. "Is berry bad," he groaned, "And too,
    I'm boring, for that if my thoughts aren't clears

"The hand not move itself, not for a few;
    No can significate for long green thing…"
    "Stop it! Stop it!" I sobbed; I whirled and threw   410.

My arms about the Bard.   "Can suffering
    Amend for aught?   To wrench the gift of speech
    From one will scant appeasement bring."

"The students judge them based on how they teach.
    I just work here.   I'll tell you what; I'll lift   415.
    His spell awhile.   Discuss it each to each."

Th' entangled spoke.   "I wonder if you'd shift
    The scene a minute while you're at it.   No?
    Well, half a loaf…   I'm flattered that you're miffed

"At what they've done to me, but what you sow,   420.
    You reap.   I fertilized the weeds the same
    As roses.   What my harvest was, you know.

"I speak, and what comes out fills me with shame,
    An echo of the deeper grief that sticks
    With me; my fate is relatively tame,   425.

"Considering I did wrong none can fix:
    You never quite unlearn misinformation.
    They acted right to put me in Old Nick's

"Hotel and sentence me to contemplation.
    My torment is mnemonic, quaint, in fact: 430.
    It helps complete my moral education."

"Well, better late,"   I said, striving for tact,
    "Even post-mortem, than never, I guess.
    But how did you, the butterfly that lacked

"All trace of diligence, ever progress   435.
    To mast'ry of this pidgin strange?   You sound
    Just like – well, like a native, I confess."

"A teacher's a linguistic Daniel; round
    About are language perils held at bay.
    He stands untouched by errors that abound."   440.

"Come now," I snorted, "leave the theories, pray.
  Real Daniels start to growl and crave raw meat.
  A little pidgin rubs off ev'ry day."

"And doctors sometimes catch the ills they treat.
  So what? Conceding my example imprecise 445.
  Let me back up. Successive groups repeat

"The same old blunders, numbing as the ice
  In London's Yukon story. Soon you catch
  Yourself slipping. The warning should suffice.

"After a while my English didn't match 450.
  What others spoke, but blithely I would bluff,
  Becoming like a tailor who would patch

Up others' coats; his own fit well enough,
  Although unrav'ling here and fraying there.
  They wanted excellence? Well, that was tough. 455.

"It wouldn't hurt our tribe if we would bear
  In mind the maxim Galen's sons recall
  To minimize th' unequal risks we share:

"'*Primum, non nocere*,' or 'First of all

Don't make things worse.' The doc scrubs down with zeal

460.

To keep the chance of complications small.

"More humbly we, when bells 'tween classes peal,

Should mentally wash out our mouths with soap.

'Twere shameful if the one trusted to heal

"Instead contaminated. Well, I hope 465.

My fate will help you straighten up. 'Twould cheer

Me as down here eternally I mope."

"It's time," said Horace. "Take leave of your peer.

The jargon-spell descends on him anew,

And we've got two more stops to make down here.

470.

"Let's imitate of Noah's sons the two

Who, when they saw him drunk, left him alone.

Turning from shame, we take our exit-cue."

"I hate to run," I told the chap I'd known.

"You brought a breath of fresh air, lit'rally:" 475.

He answered, "while you've been here, no wind's blown.

"They turned the stand storm off, that normally
    Blows day and night.   I loved the change of pace.
    You'd better go.   Don't worry about me,

"For no is nothing you can do.   The dace   480.
    Drag on.   You takee noose to dem lib still:
    A low bad talk, day put you in dis prace."

I shuddered as we thrashed along.   Until
    emerging from the garden, nothing stirred;
    Then right on cue, a gale came howling shrill.   485.

Poor devils!   Although "devils" is the word,
    At least from students' standpoint.   "What next, Boss?"
    I asked.   He pointed, spoke.   "Yon carrion bird

"Should tell you that the crew we'll come across
    Will seem unsavory, so be prepared.   490.
    There lies the spring whence flows the famous sauce

"For goose and gander.   Frankly, I'm too scared
    To go there, for its magic's hard to fight.
    No matter what your age, your never spared.

"Now, puppy love's a pretty common sight   495.
   To teachers, and there's always someone who's
   Collecting scalps, not studying at night.

"The first offense – well, you recall the blues
   The *Socialite* was singing.   There you pay
   The price right then and there: the face you lose   500.

"Lets merry classroom oligarchs hold sway.
   You paint yourself into a corner, so
   You have your fun by night, and they by day.

"Where yonder spicy Ganges starts its flow
   Maenads and satyrs bathe.   Talk all you like,   505.
   But mind: it's slipp'ry everywhere you go.

"I'll stay here, as I said.   Resume your hike
   Accompanied by yonder fairy guard
   As they escort one after her third strike."

I saw the band, and took leave of my Bard.   510.
   A swagg'ring lass with glasses for a hat
   Seemed unconcerned about her fate ill-starred.

 · She flirted with the elves, as if by that
      She could evade her doom.   In double line
      They grimly marched, unmoved by come-ons pat.   515.

She saw me.   "Hi there, baby!   What's your sign?"
      "He doesn't have one," said the ranking sprite.
      "Show him our zodiac."   "The pleasure's mine,"

She bubbled.   "Now, look up.   The books they write
      Don't fit down here, you see?   What did you say   520.
      Your name was?   Now I'll have to go and bite

The bullet, learn it all again.   They play
      Some crazy tricks down here, you'll find that out.
      Weird people.   Thought I'd warn you.   Anyway,

"Well, have a look and see what It's about.   525.
      Up there's the constellation called *The Bed.*
      Now, that's not too surprising, but I doubt

"You'll guess the next one, that one overhead:
      I think it's called *The Bottle.*   Ain't it great?
      And there's *The Little Black Book,* so they said.   530.

"And look! *The Reefer*; *Phone*; *The Leer*; there's *Plate*
And *Ticket*. But my fav'rite's in the south:
Stars form a D that stands for *Heavy Date*."

The fairy sergeant called. "Hey, rest your mouth.
We're moving on." And so we did. The air   535.
Grew dry and hot, the ground cracked as from drouth.

"It's symbolism," sighed my Sibyl fail.
"How thoughtful to include a Long Dry Spell,
So we'll appreciate the party there."

I wasn't reassured: I knew too well   540.
By now the way the Planners operated.
This was the calm; ere long the storm would swell.

I drifted over to an elf and stated
My fears. "Her mood's not hard to understand,"
He whispered back. "She always overrated   545.

"Coquettishness, and built her house on sand.
She's had it now, so grant her one last fling.
Just play along; her punishment's at hand."

I nodded, thinking of th' upcoming spring,
  And catching up to her, found her subdued.   550.
  She'd seen the vultures silent on the wing.

"This isn't symbolism! I've been screwed!
  They promised me a hot tub full of meat.
  We're going back. Somebody will get sued."

The pixie crooned, "You'll get your tub, my sweet,   555.
  Just over there. As for the hov'ring fowl,
  Your totem beasts, their function is to greet

"Newcomers. Mormons, throwing in the towel,
  Almost, were cheered by seagulls, come to save
  The day; recall, the Aztecs on the prowl   560.

"Were gladdened by an eagle; even cave
  Men had their mascots, and the buzzard's yours.
  They sing not, unproductive live, and crave

"But soulless, mindless flesh, like your amours."
  "My private life's my own," she snapped, "you prude."
                   565.

  He shot back with, "The teacher that immures

"Him- or herself in fancy, to exclude
    All save one hobbyhorse, is like a cook
    Monotonously serving the same food.

"And as for prudery, young woman, look   570.
    About you when you reach the fountainhead.
    You'll find religious zealots there, who took

"Normal erotic impulse, and instead
    Of eagerly enjoying nature's boon,
    Distorted it, transmuting gold to lead: 575.

"To King James' words they sang the same old tune;
    Testosterone or tongues of fire – what sage
    Can tell the diff'rence, judging by the loon

"Possessed by either?   There, too, Marxists rage,
    The Lenin Pentecostals, those who thrive   580.
    On red or green or black books' vulgar page,

"Their conscious minds short-circuited by jive,
    Reduced to justifying urges dark,
    To criticism dead, only alive

"For tirades on their cheap opinions.   Mark   585.
    Again, you're all the same: the singles scene
    Astrologers are put in the same Ark

"As the fanatics with their thoughts unclean.
    But paradoxic'lly you'll never suffer here,
    Forever nursed by great Hypatia Queen.   590.

"'Tis at her intercession no flames sear
    Nor ghouls outrage the souls of those who cluster
    About the vitalizing font that we're

"Approaching.   Lo!   The lady comes!   The luster
    Of learning's glow, a halo round her floats;   595.
    Her lore illuminates the ones who trust her.

"Thrice happy they on whom the Martyr dotes.
    Go greet her."   "Not so fast," said I.   "I'm told
    We're at the place for those who sowed wild oats.

"I dare not further step; I know I'd fold.   600.
    Like Cleopatra's servant I, well, dream;
    I'd not escape unscathed by orgy's hold."

A clear voice rang out: "People rightly deem
   Your Horace wise, but here he was all wet:
   He sipped a bit at inspiration's stream,   605.

"But shied away from drinking deep, upset
   By what he felt, th' unsettling thrill
   That some control, and some live to regret.

"Walk unafraid to view the Muses' rill,
   And meet the Tristans and Isoldes who   610.
   Did drink it unprepared, and rue it still.

"Poetic madness benefits a few,
   The lucky ones of seasoned, toughened mind.
   The rest are ripe, but don' know what to do

"When witchcraft seizes, dominates their blind   615.
   Spots; sex, religion, politics inflame
   The brain and lead do conduct unrefined.

"For ghastly classroom hours, yes, they're to blame,
   But frenzy can't be punished, though the sprite
   Who walks with you would lynch them all the same. 630.

"He, like your Guide, has never seen the site
Where surges up the life force.   By hearsay
They fantasize, and with more heat than light

"Tell more about themselves than those who stray
Berserk from that elixir.   Come and lead   635.
The girl.   The rest of you, be on your way."

"How was it?" Horace later asked, when we'd
Been reunited.   "Not what I expected," quoth
I, "but a most instructive stop indeed.

"There *One-track Minds* complete their stunted growth,   630.
And then return above to teach renewed.
Their fervor and persuasive pow'rs are both

"Much prized up there, once they've transcended crude
And narrow strictures, though it's simpler yet
To self-correct without death's interlude.   635.

"What's that you're wearing?   Cowboy boots?"   "You bet.
Come, put 'em on.   We'll need them at our last
Encounter," said the Satirist.   "To get

"The job Hypatia cited dealings past
    With narrow-minded madmen on the Nile.   640.
    They vilified her there; when she stood fast,

Not tailoring her views to fit their style,
    They played the trump that all fanatics hold:
    They murdered her to keep them safe awhile.

"Your turn may come, if ever you're too bold   645.
    In fighting superstition, tyranny,
    Or woman's deadly enemy of old,

"Religion that condemns her if she's free.
    Hypatia, guilty of all three offenses,
    Died victim of fanatics' lunacy.   650.

"With her the list of martyr profs commences:
    Recall that Lawrence, Solzhenitsyn taught,
    And Bruno tried to bring men to their senses."

I listened as I grunted, strained and fought
    To get the boots on.   "Why'd you give me these?" 655.
    I grumbled.   He, "Well, I believe you ought

"To be prepared to face the final sleaze."
  "That bad?" I asked, surprised. "Just wait and see.
  The way is rough that leads to Hell's grandees,

"Those jailed within the Pit eternally.   660.
  Now, watch your step." I went, and heard a crunch
  Beneath my heel. My tread had crushed a 3.

"The path that leads us to the lowest bunch
  Is paved with bogus studies and statistics,
  Compiled to prove a bureaucrat's wild hunch   665.

"And pencil-pusher's dream: state-run linguistics.
  The tycoons of *Bilingual Ed.,* that kept
  The faith that spawned all sorts of language mystics,

"Are guarded there by giants twain, adept
  At governing all sorts of folly. First,   670.
  Sublime Cervantes shames their lips inept

"On one side: Shakespeare hears their well-rehearsed
  Entreaties to improve their jail with grants.
  Let's have a look, but be braced for the worst."

As when a prima donna rhythm scants,   675.
    We trampled heedless on the hapless numbers.
    Then Horace spoke again: "Roll up your pants;

"One vision more, and then you end your slumbers,
    But first we wade through an infernal stream
    That, like the river Lethe, thought encumbers: 680.

"A moat of bullshit guards the shifty team
    That begged for bread and circuses.   No shame
    At all they felt when telling the regime,

" 'Ignore the fact that other nations came
    To these fair shores and learned their English well   685.
    Before our pipe dreams had a catchy name;

" 'Ignore the fact that we can scarcely spell
    In Spanish, that our jerky jargon jars
    The Spanish-speaking world from which we fell;

" 'Just give us millions; make us look like stars.   690.
    You want the votes, we want prestige; if you
    Throw us a bone, we'll keep you as our czars.

" 'There will be those who take the narrow view,
    That since no Yiddish, Czech, Vietnamese
    Or Greek endeavors have been lobbied through,   695.

" 'They might conclude   we come here on our knees
    Because we think our people aren't as bright
    As others.   Let them think whate'er they please;

" 'Despite the evidence, we feel we're right.
    Besides, we'll go to bat for you, and sweep   700.
    Real issues 'neath the rug and out of sight,

" 'To keep our folk politically asleep.
    You'll reign forever, free to bilk and steal
    The country blind while we rein in the sheep.' "

We grimly sloshed along.   "Although I'd feel   705.
    No greater thrill," I ventured, "than to meet
    The noblest pens of England and Castile,

"The ordure's depth must signify defeat:
    We'd need hip boots if we're to reach the shore,
    Or Moses, who could make the tide retreat."   710.

My Leader nodded.   "We can wade no more.
   We really need a boat; but understand
   That no one's ever been squeamish before.

"For pilgrims bound for yonder promised land
   'Tis mother's milk we're in.   To fertilize   715.
   Careers with it, 'twas always close at hand.

"Like dolphins that cavort 'neath Carib skies
   They frolic in their element, then tired
   But happy they attain the strand where lies

"Their happy hunting ground.   Refreshed, inspired   720.
   And glowing from their dip, they inland race
   To meet their destiny.   Now, we, here mired,

"Must or resolve to follow or retrace
   Our steps, unless.. unless we fly!   Behold,
   On churning wings the guardian of the place,   725.

"The Gerrymander hither hies, the old
   Accomplice of the parasites that sunder
   Apart whole towns to keep them in the fold.

"We'll ask him for a lift." Above the thunder
    Of flapping pinion boomed its raucous tone: 730.
    "Ho, sluggards! Hesitate ye? Why, I wonder,

"Stand ye bequalmed, the first guests that I've known
    To need encouragement... A live one! How
    Did you get here?" "Fair dragon, though I own

"His presence is irregular, I vow   735.
    No mischief's meant," the Puglian said. "To end
    Our journey we require assistance now.

"So I beseech you, mighty snake, to lend
    That great broad back of yours to help us gain
    Firm footing, that I may return my friend   740.

"In time for class tomorrow, if the strain
    Is not too great for you." "Don't make me laugh,"
    The serpent sneered. "For years I've borne a train

"Of donkeys, elephant herds too, to staff
    State houses o'er the nation. Hop aboard.   745.
    You'll whisk along as swift as wind-blown chaff,

"But leave your boots behind."   We did and toward
   The distant terra firma streaked.   The beast
   Soon circled o'er the isle beyond the ford.

Below we saw the scavenging deceased   750.
   Like ants, but milling round, as when the hill
   Hears of a carcass near on which to feast.

Our monster spiraled gently down, until
   We saw their glitt'ring eyes, their snarls we caught.
   "You'll note they're very territorial still,"   755.

Said Horace, "but if we're wary we ought
   To reconnoiter safely.   Worm, alight!
   We'll view the fiefdom double talk has bought."

I'll never know the rest.   My chanticleer
   Alarm clock roused me, dragged me by the ear   760.
   From Pluto's palace and its torments drear.
   Interpret you my glimpse of Hell's frontier
   As best you can.   The travelog ends here.

Envoy

When dreams possess us, eagerly we mark
Details and later ponder what they meant.   765.
Our minds illuminate us in the dark;
We cherish insights by th' unconscious sent.

Yet waking we ignore the lessons plain
Our senses pass along: we tune them out,
As if afraid to trust our daytime brain.   770.
We hesitate and grope, made dull by doubt.

For most of us it's noon, or afternoon,
High time to be astir, and be in turn
Enlightened by the sun as well as moon.
They both reveal endless lessons to learn.   775.

Use, then, both spheres to guide you on your way,
And be an owl by night, a hawk by day.

Noon

Prof. Forceps runneth to Prof. Malleus

Forceps.   I got your note and came straightway.   What's wrong?
    You're pale and shaking.   Can this be the same
    Stout heart that vowed to undertake a long
    Housecleaning to restore his tarnished name?
    Speak up, man!   Tell me what afflicts you so.   5.
    We'll find a remedy.   Come on, then, why so low?

Malleus.   I came to class just brimming with elan,
    But found a golden calf enthronéd there:
    Foul mutiny did thwart my lesson plan.
    Instead of irrigating deserts bare   10.
    I struggled to cut down, as best I might,
    A bedlam jungle that had sprung up overnight.

Polite appeals for order went unheeded.
    Stallion nor mare would near the water go,
    But frisked and kicked and finally stampeded.   15.
    They vied to strike the most unkindest blow,
    Not just the shiftless ones: quick to rebel,
    My pets had beat their plowshares into swords as well.

Forceps.   I'll give you no advice (I never do),
    But offer you my shoulder and my ear.   20.
    Let's get a box of Kleenex and a brew
    And talk it out.   Solutions will appear.
    To prime the pump, a secret shall I show:
    My will, that I, depressed, set down some time ago.

In Taberna

Forceps.   Well, here it is.   I, Forceps, three decades   25.
    And two years old, my mind still sound in spite
    Of coping with my students' escapades,
    My testament with my own hand I write.
    My lawyer says to disinherit those
    Not named below; all right.   Having done that, here goes.
                                        30.

Malleus. Good. Bismillah. What's there? What do I get?
A whip and chair? Or some blunt instrument?

Forceps. Just hold your horses, ace; I'm not dead yet.
To give you thoughts, not things, is my intent.

Malleus. Forgive me. I'm still rattled. I don't need   35.
Gadgets or props, but fresh ideas. My friend, proceed.

Forceps. Rather than read the whole megillah through,
Let's borrow Bruno's tart taxonomy:
Describe the rogues that make your class a zoo.
We'll deal with them in groups and sev'rally.   40.
I'll pick and choose the items that relate
To your dilemma 'mong bequests from my estate.

Malleus. Though agonizing to recount the sack
Of what was once Minerva's citadel,
For you I'll list the leaders of the pack,   45.
The captains of the siege, their tactics fell.
Awake, my saint John Barleycorn, my lay,
Since Crispian seems elsewhere on this shameful day.

An antidote for mercury, perhaps,
Would help the first inmate that comes to mind.   50.

Now frenzy unrestrained, then quick relapse
To torpor and defeatism, combined
With little aptitude for learning, make
His corner of the room a blight when he's awake;

That's *Takdir al-Mektub,* always at sea,   55.
But doldrum bound, his TOEFL progress dead
Because of Zionist conspiracy,
He blandly says, and shrugs and shakes his head.
The deck of life is stacked: thy will be done.
I offer learning tips; he nods,   but takes not one.   60.

But hard it is to patiently await
The moment Destiny decides he'll score.
His passions seethe at times; you cant make Fate
A nervous wreck, but what are teachers for?
He dormant waits until I've dropped my guard,   65.
Then suddenly erupts, leaving me drained and scarred.

Forceps.   plan an ambush on requires a lull.
How sure are you you're being brisk and bright?
It seems to me, to rev up such a skull
Takes peace and quiet.   Your job's to excite.   70.
Eye contact is the spark to build a fire
Beneath bench-warmers, or at least make them perspire.

But no, you're mesmerized by books or notes.
    Let's free you up to stare them down or give
    Encouragement; now one drills, now one dotes,   75.
    And doesn't miss a beat.   Think cup, not sieve.
    Intensity's the thing.   Make him respond;
    If not to language, grip him in a simpler bond.

Now the bequest, to tide you over till
    You're rational enough to see this rout   80.
    Instead of Armageddon, Bunker Hill;
    You've lost, but you've a future to plan out.
    The Sufis say, "Seek wisdom, go as far
    As China," but halfway is where the treasures are.
    A guidebook to a Balkan stronghold see.   85.

Malleus.   Those Bulgar soirees that are all the rage?
Forceps.   Though that would do, the gate of ivory
    Will only get you to a certain stage.
    I grant these language seances are chic,
    And hordes of scholars now a happy medium seek;   90.

But as for me, I've better things to do
    Than watching groggy students slouch and sigh.
    What trance taught Junior how to tie his shoe?
    What swimmer learned his skill benumbed and dry?

It may be that truth comes in reverie: 95.
The tooth fairy, though, never brought enough for me.

Like Faust, I play with fire, invoke the muse
    That's brought more mischief to our age than joy,
    I speak of oratory.   Scoundrels use
    It; why can't decent folks its pow'rs employ?   100.

Malleus.   I'll hold my nose an give your plan a try.
    Which rascal's ravings least enrage, most edify?

Forceps.   Seek Yugoslavia.   Let the Bulgars nap.
    The Singer of Tales read between the lines
    Will teach you ready eloquence, and tap   105.
    Pow'rs none save child of Orpheus divines.
    You'll parry their crude sallies with this text
    And lord it over troublemakers.   Well, who's next?

Malleus.   In midst of being butch and businesslike,
    I find myself distracted by the pose   110.
    Luz Cazapantalones deigns to strike.
    The Jezebel gets to me, and she knows.
    I crave none of Adonis' manly grace,
    But his detachment; I know lust is on my face.

Catullus' idol made his vision dim,   115.
His ears buzz and his limbs all wobbly by
Her wit as much as beauty.   Unlike him,
I've a Delilah who is merely sly.
What, short of Attys' cure, will help me stay
My wand'ring mind, and buttress up my feet of clay?
                                                                    120.
What says your testament?

Forceps.   Here's a bequest
To buck you up: two tickets.

Malleus.   Bound for where?

Forceps.   Theater tickets.

Malleus.   Shows that are addressed
To language teachers?   That seems morbid fare.

Forceps.   Lord, save us from the guild mentality!   125.
You're first a human being; second, employee.

Todd Browning's *Freaks*, seen once, should do the trick
To cure your voyeuristic tendencies.
Dumb longing for a guy or gal who's slick

Shows childish values, warped priorities.   130.
Professional development is fine,
But, if you're not together, pearls before the swine.

And, lest the pendulum should swing too wide,
    The next will teach compassion for the brain
    Behind that gorgeous face, the heart inside   135.
    The body; *Born Yesterday* tells it plain.
    Let others gape medusaed; forge you on,
    Producing language wizard, mental amazon.

Malleus.   A movie ticket!   How unorthodox.
Forceps.   The question's if, not how you crack the nut,   140.
    Or where you find it.   Portia's golden box
    And your experience both yield gems uncut.
    Not hidden, but encoded are the keys
    That get you to our art's enciphered mysteries.

I'm giving you no system petrified,   145.
    No groc'ry list, no recipe at all;
    I want to make you hungry, not to tide
    You over till next time you drop the ball.
    I want to nudge you till you leave the nest
    And forage for yourself.   Let's take up your next pest.
                                                        150.

Malleus.   Behold *Juan Perez Oso.*, five-toed sloth:
   He brings to class naught but a limpid grin.
   No matter how I plead and prance and froth,
   My yang's too puny for his boundless yin.
   Unmoved, he treats my threats and blandishments,   155.
   Though amiably, with bodhisattva diffidence.

I wonder why he scorns the saffron robe;
   The rest is there: th' unfurrowed brow, suggesting
   Like dearth of wrinkles on his frontal lobe.
   He may be in Nirvana, or just resting.   160.
   Thus out of space and time, he's never known
   Fear of rebirth as cow or pig or anglophone.

Forceps.   Let saints, not students in a stupa sit.
   Instead of burning incense, smoke him out.
   On Borobudur's crest let angels flit;   165.
   Up there the lotus has no chance to sprout.
   He might be just a lotus-eater, one
   Preferring "lotus" ripened 'neath Colombia's sun.

Assume he's sober, and his brain intact;
   He's numb above, so hit below the belt,   170.
   Just hard enough to get him to react.
   A tap or two will make your interest felt.

Reverse the Gurkha's oath: what I bequeath –
Now swear! – must be returned unbloodied to its sheath.

A newspaper I leave you, not to swat   175.
    Him with;   it's kindling to ignite the trash
    Between his ears. 'Twill find the friction-spot
    Where sparks fly when conflicting values clash.
    "Just living" 's an ideal that dulls him, true;
    But "Dying for the fatherland" might pull him through.
                         180.

As wolves race toward an almost empty fold,
    Knowing full well the sheepdog's on his way,
    So Argentines would leave their *maté* cold,
    Thirsty instead for glory, spoils and sway.
    Throughout the world expatriates raised Cain;   185.
    Descamisados brought Peron to life again.

Book Seven of th' *Aeneid* was replayed.
    Notice the backdrop of the drama sad,
    The ardor of the pawns that were betrayed,
    Their willingness to swallow slogans mad.   190.
    Their tyrants waved the flag, and off they went.
    This blind spot is their grief; for you its heaven-sent.

Retain the means, improve the ends.   In place
   Of pouring talent down a rathole, propping
   Up dictators or flags or church or race,   195.
   His harvest is his own: he's not sharecropping.
   But wean him slow; good soldier Schweik won't quit
   His dumb act overnight: he'll do it bit by bit.

Your questions, though, must be the wedge to crack
   His hibernation: Don't students prepare   200.
   For class in Ecuador?   Are scholars slack
   In Chile, caring but to flirt and stare?
   The answer's no, of course.   Back off, and purr
   Encouragement at his first steps. and spare the spur.

Malleus.   That takes a lot of nerve.

Forceps.   It takes compassion.   205.
   Look at him, diagnose, roll up your sleeves
   And roust him from his hammock.

Malleus.   But the fashion
   Seems risky.

Forceps.   So it is.   He who believes
   The Stoic creed recalls a dictum: When

You stir the mud, it stinks.　Be braced for fragrance, then.
　　　　　　　　　　　　　　　　　　210.

Next.

Malleus.　*Hassan al-Tahshish*, whose calling card
　　　Has Franklin's picture on it, wouldn't miss
　　　My class for anything, nor finds it hard
　　　To choose 'tween learning and his houri's kiss.
　　　He does his best for me, but I hear tell　　　215.
　　　Our female colleagues want him in a padded cell.

His extramural odalisques behave,
　　　But not the brazen hussy who, unveiled,
　　　Acts like a teacher, not a pretty slave.
　　　His offer to assume the sceptre failed;　　　220.
　　　His paynim sense of order thus outraged
　　　A multi-fronted *jihad* has he 'gainst her waged.

The odds are bad:　she's obviously gay,
　　　Since burning glances melt her not, nor does
　　　His shirt unbuttoned take her breath away.　　　225.
　　　Even tight pants are vain, as is chin fuzz.
　　　Medallions mighty, shoes of mirror shine,
　　　And torrents of cologne work not to make her pine.

His sense of duty drives him on.   A night
   Of love would straighten the virago out;   230.
   He'd do the therapy, to be polite.
   To wear her down, he'll sneer and leer and pout,
   And fire her secret longing for his touch
   Through jealousy; his female classmates won't mind much.

And he'll expose the weakness of her mind   235.
   By sternly pointing out discrepancies
   Between her grammar and the sort you find
   When English is enriched across the seas
   By arabesques, whose depth is o'er her head;
   Correction's needed, lest his classmates be misled.   240.

With interruptions, tardiness and sass
   The strategy's complete, the war is on.
   What have you got to help our comrade pass
   The gauntlet through, when battle lines are drawn?
Forceps.   Quoth Aristotle: If women are cheated,   245.
   Half of the human race lives frustrated, defeated.

I've thought a lot about this.   I confess
   I draw a blank.   That's it   I've no insights
   Or formulas to counteract the mess
   Our trade is in, where half of us have rights,   250.

Others, what's left.   For what can counteract
The machinations of a worldwide macho pact?

As hypocrites South Africa malign,
    As if our own blacks lived in paradise;
    As Carter dropped Brazil a scorching line,   255.
    Then threw the Shah a dinner party twice;
    A writer's jailed, we treat him like a saint;
    When nations grind their women down, it's merely quaint.

Hypocrisy above, treason behind:
    Their sisters stab them in the back.   Some sell
    Themselves for cash, some for religion blind,
    Resentful of   the women who do well.
    I'm stumped.   A bigger brain than mine must kill
    The vicious circle that enslaves both Jack and Jill.

Malleus.   Three out of four's not bad.

Forceps.   And not enough.   265.
    But let's get back to you.   Who else resists
    Your pedagogic efforts, gives you guff?

Malleus.   *Shlemo bar-Sheygits* constantly insists
    On TOEFL, and bedevils me to chuck

All else; if not, to let him be and wish him luck.   270.

He hunches o'er his torah, nor is tempted
    By talmud I offer.   I call on him
    To speak in class; he feels that he's exempted
    From recitations and *melamed*'s whim.
    One candle brightens his menorah bare,   275.
    His *dreydl* has but one side to attract his stare.

Hello?

Forceps.   Oh, sorry.   My mind drifted back
    To that *Tahshish.*

Malleus.   Let's let my scoundrels rest,
    And focus on a good plan of attack.

Forceps.   A deus ex machina for her hard-pressed.

Malleus.   You got a light?

Forceps.   Here.

Malleus.   Mehercule!   The flame!
    A woman's face floats in it!   Spirit, speak your name.

Spirit.   Camilla visits you, the warrior maid.

    I'm touched to see you big strong men concerned,

    Grieved at the double standard you've displayed.   285.

    I'll give you straight the gist of what I've learned.

    Look in the mirror; trip him up with smarts:

    Dress British, think Yiddish.   He's licked before he starts.

Malleus.   She had a gift for terseness, don't you think?

    A double standard?

Forceps.   That's why I was stumped.   290.

    The problem is extreme, but there's a link

    With what I said before.   I should have jumped

    On the solution; I was blind, of course.

    Women's and men's teaching strengths come from the same source.

Look in the mirror: see what students see.   295.

    If fear, learn judo; if depression's there,

    Dig deep and come up smiling; coquetry?

    Then button up your blouse and brush your hair.

    Suspicion?   Bitterness?   Need for support?

    Junk that.   Show them that teaching is your fav'rite sport.

                                  300.

A healthy wariness must be your shield;
Be braced for mischief.   Let your helmet be
Foresight.   Be fluency the sword you wield.
Your breastplate a clear conscience, tarnish-free.
A targe emblazoned with your int'rests wide   305.
Will warn them not to waste the time you've set aside

For teaching, that you've bigger fish to fry.
A strong front will transform his useless lust
To puppy love: a godsend, for he'll try
His best to shine, and shrink from your disgust.   310.
Faust 's my bequest.   The spirit that denies
Is purged by woman's magic, made refined and wise.

Where were we?

Malleus.   *Bar-Sheygits.*

Forceps.   Before we pry
Him loose, recall, the book he's married to
Is not so bad.   He shouldn't put it by   315.
To please a jealous martinet or shrew.
Seduce him with your zeal and well-planned course,
Then scold him now and then for beating a dead horse.

Many's the time a textbook's compensated
   For teacher's lack of int'rest, brains and ears.   320.
   A book's asylum for th' intimidated,
   A comfort for their fantasies and fears.
   An open volume's oft an SOS
   From timid students.   They're the ones we'll next address.

Malleus.   Poor *Hazukashi-san* is smart, but scared.   325.
   I call on her, she seems to blow a fuse.
   She whispers – she would murmur if she dared –
   And right or wrong, she gazes at her shoes.
   I coax   her, compliment her should she squeak
   An answer out.   No dice.   I've sought a new technique.
          330.

Try rescuing a kitten from a tree
   When you don't even know that tree it's in.
   I've tried t' approach the problem cult'rally,
   In Pasiphae's wise her heart to win:
   I practiced bowing, shucked shoes at the door.
   I studied sumo, sumi, too, kimonos wore;   335.

No tempura was safe with me around;
   I haunted sam'rai flicks, thrice *Shogun* read;

My jogging tapes featured *okoto*'s sound;
Shunned coffee, drank that funny tea instead.   340.
So far this hasn't helped *H.-san*, but I'm
Enjoying it: I've never had such a grand time.

What does she know?   I'm obviously right.
The vested int'rests in the field say so.
Ergo, if she's not swept away, it's spite.   345.
Case closed.   She'll come around, or elsewhere go.
My colleagues' criticism hurt at first,
But since I've tuned them out, why, let them do their worst.

Forceps.   Spare me your armchair anthropology!
You skim a culture like a pebble skips
Across the water, and pretend you see   350.
What others don't.   Our trade relationship's
Secure enough for me to give rebuttal:
That ev'ry decent teacher does this, but it's subtle.

As Sinon brought about the fall of Troy
By crafty speech, so you can breach the wall   355.
By sympathetic use of language ploy,
And gently blow her cool once and for all.
The rule's compassion.   You're sunk if you ever
Try to be clever for the sake of being clever.

If she's blasé about the local "joo,"   360.
   A "dojo" shows you care, and sets her straight.
   A query that begins by asking "fho"
   Elicits "swe firo" to clean the slate,
   "Ooman," "Ooatak'shi-ooa."   A "sameful" loss?
   A "do itasimaste" gets your point across.

How strong is your commitment?   Go whole hog
   Or drop it now, not shrinking from the rest.
   You see the rising sun peep through the fog,
   But don't neglect the morning calm.   Each guest
   Deserves the same: the middle, free or south   370.
   Lands have an equal claim on teacher's ears and mouth.

You've just admitted that your class contains
   The Cid's descendants and the twain offspring
   Of Abraham.   Who else?   Will you take pains
   To see that no one's slighted, no group's king?   375.
   Your dedication to how well you teach
   Will plunge you in, or keep you wading near the beach.

Malleus.   So no bequests?

Forceps.   For form's sake, let me toss
   A couple off: chrestomathies and tapes

To give you pow'r, and keep you at a loss: 380.
Strong wine to sip, and taste of sour grapes.
Add Kafka's *Burrow* for the bookworm.   While
Were in the East, what other problems are on file?

Malleus.   Comrade *Wang Pagui* 's catalepsy's broken
By outbursts at the mention of his land.   385.
He's death on ambiguities, outspoken
Lest running dogs' slanders get out of hand
He comes out swinging till he's asked to read,
Then goes inscrutable, no matter how I plead.

In short, if it's not propaganda, naught   390.
Inspires him to hold forth.   The Gang of Four
Is good for a philippic, and the thought
Of the Long March fails not to make him soar
Lin Piao's betrayal's worthy of his pen,
All else nonexistent, foreign as Sun Yat Sen.   395.
Well?

Forceps.   Feed the fire, but make sure that it spreads
To praise of homely things.   Keep pressing till
You strike the bedrock common to the reds
And other folks.   Let him indulge in shrill
Paeans to dogs inspired by Chairman Mao   400.

That warn them of earthquakes by setting up a row.

Intrigue him, pique his curiosity:
How do these dogs convey their premonition?
They don't "wang-wang" in English, usually.
Supply him with proverbs for ammunition.   405.
"His bark's worse than his bite;" a train of crumbs
Like these addicts him to daily verbal dim sums.

One doesn't stop express trains on a dime,
Nor do they make turns of ninety degrees.
Concede his drive, and harness it to climb   410.
Parnassus' crest by morsels such as these.
Poor Richard's Almanac   I leave you; plain
Wisdom, tartly expressed: homely bait for his brain.

Malleus.   You've yet to tell me what I learned in school.
Was it for naught I studied trends and fads   415.
And kept a notebook on each modish tool
And learned great names?   Were all these fellows cads?
Why do you shun the standard tactics?   Are
They all so bad you trust none as a guiding star?

Forceps.   Transmission equals decadence.   No matter   420.
How hot th' idea was, when simplified

Enough to be passed on, it winds up flatter,
Less flexible and rich, oft misapplied.
Bandy about no pioneer's good name
To dignify your travesties that bring him shame.   425.

Filch not his reputation: it may be
     You cornered him at a convention, but
     That doesn't make you spokesman instantly;
     He autographed the book that you keep shut,
     But is he honored by name-dropping glib?   430.
     By being cited just to glamorize a fib?

It may be that the law I'm laying down
     May be bereft of context, vulgarized,
     Accepted by hearsay and used to crown
     Abuses that I've elsewhere criticized.   435.
     My curse on those who paraphrase my word,
     Apologies to those upset by what they've heard.

I'm raving.   Back to you: we'll cultivate
     Our garden, fertilize and weed it clean.

Malleus.   Let's deal with *Troi Mu Nguyen,* a bit of freight
                                                      440.
     Entrusted to Hanoi's merchant marine.

He's very bright, which probably is why
The commies towed him out to sea, hoping he'd die.

He's doing well, but his Achilles' heel
    Is speech: diphthongs and consonants fall prey   455.
    To his monosyllabifying zeal.
    The quacking sounds that on his lips do play
    Are so far off the mark I've had no luck
    In rectifying how he talks, so we're both stuck.

To make things worse,   the goons in class respond   450.
    To his singsong with coarse hilarity.
    Impervious to shame they snort, beyond
    The reach of even basic decency.
    Ong Nguyen sometimes clams up, and sometimes growls,
    But his come-backs elicit only louder howls.   455.

In oafish wise, when they want to take five,
    "Tek bek" is how these beasts request a pause.
    Similar kennings grace their barb'rous jive,
    Yet they are stung when I point out their flaws.
    Troi Mu, bewildered, grumpy, turns to me   460.
    To still the swirling storm and calm the raging sea.

Forceps.   ll ask three questions.   First, can you be sure
    You haven't been haphazard in your coaching?
    He's talented, so if you find him poor
    In one respect, be ruthless in approaching   465.
    His weak point; be relentless, patient, too.
    Start early and don't flinch until his accent's true.

Next, is your nagging aimed at one and all?
    The pitfall of our trade's a deadened ear.
    Beware when French accents cease to appall,   470.
    Or Persian drawls no longer seem so queer.
    Your class drifts like a ship without a rudder
    The minute any brogue no longer makes you shudder.

To make your jeremiads sound sincere
    Let no one be complacent or immune.   475.
    If they've arrived, what are they doing here?
    If like rules touch both pet and pantaloon,
    They should back off.   A sense of sympathy
    Will get them off their classmate's back permanently.

Query the third: assuming all is square,   480.
    Why be surprised that after ten offenses
    The others gnash their teeth and tear their hair?
    They lack your patience, since they pay th' expenses.

Here's Roberts' *Rules of Order* for the horde;
You should take all the voice lessons you can afford. 485.

Malleus.　Voice lessons?　As in singing?

Forceps.　He who taps
　　　　Italian wisdom learns first-hand the skill
　　　　Of rectifying tongues and throats and chaps,
　　　　Finds tricks it's taken cent'ries to distill.
　　　　Singing's extension of your normal speech;　　490.
　　　　Tinker with one, you'll find the other in your reach.

Apart from understanding how it feels
　　　　To modify the talking muscles, know
　　　　Teachers who swallow words or talk in squeals
　　　　Will undercut their pow'r to make things flow.　　495.
　　　　You do sit-ups to keep your waistline slim,
　　　　So exercise your voice to stay in fighting trim.

Malleus.　You mentioned mime when last we talked.

Forceps.　Beware
　　　　Lest you forget they're opposites.　Increase
　　　　Your magnetism by mime's pow'r to pare　　500.
　　　　Away distracting gestures, till you cease

Your random flutter and no more rely
On dumb-show tricks or hula handwork to get by.

I've got to get to class.   Accompany
   Me and we'll figure out the rest of these   505.
   You've locked horns with.

Malleus.   I know I'm not home free.
   I face twelve toils in all.

Forceps.   Like Hercules.
   We've talked of eight; the other four describe
   And we'll decide how best to quell your mut'nous tribe.

But mark, description's little worth unless   510.
   You follow through and face the problem squarely,
   Determined to clean up th' Augean mess,
   To soothe the Hydra you confront, and fairly.
   Pandora knew the trick to close the lid
   Of her notorious box.   A lot of good that did.   515.

Minutiae will do you little good:
   Macbeth consulted with no botanist
   For genus, species found in Birnam Wood
   When leafy legions marched out of the mist.

No matter how detailed your data gleam,   520.
Unless on target, friend, you're living in a dream.

Malleus.   When *Reza Ramazani* staggered in
For his first class day, inly I debated
Whether or not t' ascribe his gait to gin
Or some disease that left him enervated.   525.
He'd wanly sit, and when I'd say, "Recite!"
His answer was, "I can't.   I didn't sleep last night."

What specialist, I wondered, should he see?
His symptoms: dizziness and torpor, loss
Of appetite, irritability,   530.
The air of one who's killed an albatross.
I asked a doctor friend, who chuckled, "You
Will see complete recov'ry when the moon is new."

"I asked Hypocrates, Ptolemy spoke,"
I testily rejoined, but right on cue   535.
The night the crescent showed, his "fever" broke.
Shamefaced, I asked my pal just how he knew.
"One needs no med school, no astrology.
This was the Muslim's holy month," he said to me.

"I'll never understand," I heard him say,   540.
   "Why these guys sign up for a course when it's
   Supposed to be a time to fast and pray.
   They sleepwalk, and it gives their teachers fits.
   Expect the same until Allah sublime
   On Judgment Day calls to account the waste of time."
                                         545.

Forceps.   I've never seen it work, but feel I owe
   It to my class to point out that their are
   Exceptions to the mandate: 'gainst the foe
   No soldier's touched, as long as there's a war.
   Embroiled in conquest, they are warriors, too.   550.
   No truce, no quarter for the tongue that they pursue.

It always fails.   Each year I see the toll
   Their daily deprivation takes, and how
   Learning's displaced by a more visc'ral goal:
   Another day sans girls, smokes, booze or chow.   555.
   Bootless t' ascribe their acts to faith or folly,
   Crucial, before the month starts, that you've got their lolly.

Dispassionately, once the checks have cleared,
   You can decide whether to let them drift
   Or spoon-feed them with easy questions steered   560.

In their direction, to give them a lift.

On no account let your momentum die,

Nor stall the convoy just because one tank is dry.

My *Golden Bough* will cheer you when I'm gone,

    'Twill check the impulse to get off the track   565.

By spending class time counting angels on

Pinheads, and hold your criticism back.

You'll read how far we've come, and shake no finger

At harmless relics of the Stone Age that still linger.

The hazy zone 'twixt fact and superstition's   570.

    A given in our trade.   Let laissez-faire

As principle confine your intuitions,

Nor see yourself as a poor man's Voltaire.

Ben Franklin had it right when he'd advise

Caution when touching someone's credit, creed or eyes.

    575.

Stick to your trade and you'll command respect;

    Go off on tangents and you're on thin ice.

Esteem's a two-way street.   Uncircumspect

Pontificating's just not worth the price.

Enough of this.   Let's grapple with some more   80.

Of your bad apples, ere we reach my classroom door.

Malleus. I've figured out *Sorah Bonbasti* 's reason
    For wearing a babushka every day:
    It insulates her head from Satan's treason,
    And keeps her guard up, lest the C.I.A.   585.
    Entice her, as an agent in disguise
    Once caused Eve's fall. She irritates and mystifies.

Thus shielded by her scarf and neutral smock
    She takes cheap shots at everything that moves,
    And cherishes her deep-felt culture shock   590.
    As if it were a medal, since it proves
    The wickedness around her's failed to stain
    Her smugness or infect with doubt her sterile brain.

Forceps. Lie down with dogs and you'll rise up with fleas,
    The proverb goes, and holds for infidel   595.
    Dogs too. You see no symptoms of disease,
    Only the quarantine's protective shell.
    In time she'll find that no protection works
    Against the Yankeeitis that within her lurks.

Although contagious, there's a dormant phase   600.
    Where all seems normal. Years from now, back home,
    Though kept under close observation, praise
    For ancient ways grows fainter. The syndrome

Then suddenly flares up.   Her glassy eye
Grows thoughtful, and her neighbors catch her asking "why?"

Malleus.   Having the last laugh wasn't what I had
In mind.   It gives me confidence, but how
Do I beat back her daily raids a tad?
Thank you, I'll take my mess of pottage now,
Circle the wagons, form a square, entrench,   610.
And count the days until I'm rid of that vile wench.

Forceps.   Outflank her with this item from my will:
A Koran well-translated puts the shoe
On th' other foot; her shame will keep her still,
And it ties in with English-learning, too.   615.
These Muslims really don't know their book well,
So offhand questions, you'll find, stun them for a spell.

Idly remark, "A Jonah is a cat
Who brings… well, Sorah, what?" and "If one hears
Of Solomonic wisdom, what is that?"
Reading O. Henry's Christmas tale, appears
The Queen of Sheba, and so on.   She'll need
To don her thinking cap; teach freely while she's treed.

She'll come to dread the formulaic tag
   "That's in the Koran, right" as saucer-eyed   625.
   She racks her brains in vain, forgets to nag.
   Then, though you'll never have her on your side,
   You being Satan's spawn and all, she'll take
   Her ranting somewhere else and give your ears a break.

Malleus.   Didn't you say you give it to them straight?   630.

Forceps.   Give what?

Malleus.   "Gift of the Magi."

Forceps.   Sure, don't you?

Malleus.   It's hard.   My goal's to teach, not to frustrate.

Forceps.   I don't believe my ears.   A vital clue
   Is this.   Now listen.   If you give them junk
   To read, that oversimplifed stuff, man, you're sunk.
                       635.
   Charisma, crowd control are fine at first,
   But they crave meat; no skill can check their wiles
   When, bestialized by boredom, crazed by thirst
   For data, mischief lurks beneath their smiles.

So, push them.   Give them something they can chew;
                                                                640.
They'll sink their teeth into the book, or into you.

Let's let this rest until next time we meet,
    And get our present topic squared away.
    At our next rendezvous we'll textbooks treat.
    Hoe your row to the end, I always say.   645.
    We'll keep on trolling.   You still have a pair
Of ogres, if I count right, that we've still to snare.

Malleus.   My most accomplished learner now plays possum,
    Bogged down by language cargo she's amassed.
    Marie-Francine Panneseche, the hybrid blossom   650.
    Of seeds sown in her land's colonial past,
    Caught 'twixt th' uncompromising fleur-de-lis
And Afric tongues as complex as the baobab tree,

Is just worn out.   Dozens of lingos thrive
    In Iv'ry Coast, this ebon maiden's soil.   655.
    She's mastered eight or nine, but lost her drive,
    Too conscious of each one's required toil.
    Now English haunts her like Dimitri's ghost,
And, like Tsar Boris, rest is what she wants the most.

French is her crutch, her harbor on the breaks: 660.
    A synonym for "fair" ?   It's iron, of course;
    When words get Saxon, why she gets the shakes,
    Seeks out her pals and puckers till she's hoarse.
    Back to the salt mines, then, devoid of charm.
    The Russians may make English just a false alarm,   665.

So wait and see.   What if they do?   The game
    Begins again: *krovat'* will then acquire
    "Necktie" for synonym; things stay the same
    The more they change.   What's needed to inspire
    The slumming francophile to taste, at least,   670.
    The courses set before her at our language feast?

Now that I think of it, her plight ties in
    With *Rani Bandobastpur* 's double bind.
    Her speech is clear to her Gangetic kin,
    A riddle to the rest of humankind.   675.
    Her words descend like hailstones on the ear.
    She shrieks as though she wanted folks back home to hear.

She senses something's wrong, but won't adjust.
    I tell her, though Sanskrit's daughters demand
    An adamantine jaw, eftsoons she must   680.
    Slack off and imitate our diction bland;

Since we speak crisply only when we scold,
More soothing tones must out, else she'll leave people cold.

Forceps.   And does she straight effect the change you've sought?

Malleus.   No way.

Forceps.   I'm not surprised.   I've always found   685.
    Your Hindu a linguistic juggernaut,
    And with good reason, since his grammar's sound
    And his vocabulary's downright vast.
    With so much on their side, no wonder they stand fast.

I'll offer a suggestion to expand   690.
    Her consciousness of speaking styles, without
    Belittling what she learned in Bharat-land;
    Send her to films you can sincerely tout
    As top-notch entertainment, but present
    Her ears with challenges to make her time well-spent.
                    695.

The Commonwealth's a movie buff's gold mine,
    And diff'rent accents cause a piquant strain
    To exercise the ear.   Northward the Nine
    (Though dragging a bilingual ball and chain)

Enchant Canadian cameras; southwest,   700.
New Zealand's few films must be counted with the best.

Then, 'cross the Tasman Sea invite their eyes:
The foreign movies that I've most enjoyed,
That grip me quick, and bear frequent reprise,   705.
Come from the new princess of celuloid:
Australian films are something to respect,
And they provide the acid test of dialect.

Malleus.   The francophile?

Forceps.   Recall, the ravens fed
Elijah, not vice versa.   Students bring
The lust to learn; if they show scorn instead,   710.
How, then, can you supply the hankering?
And yet, she's laid her money down, which shows
Some appetite; her nonchalance is just a pose.

Hang on.   My will contains a clause germane
To those stymied by pride.   No, here are two: 715.
My tackle box and rod and reel, to gain
The short-term qualities to get you through
The day; from anglers learn to cultivate
Skill at enticing and th' ability to wait.

Item the second, geared for the long haul,   720.
    Will reinforce decisiveness, and keep
    Your concentration sharp,   maintain withal
    A light touch and light heart when things get steep:
    A grab bag with my fencing foil and bike,
    My wei-chi set, my telescope, flute and such-like. 725.

Diversions that refresh and keep you sharp,
    Since you must lead the class in sanity,
    Are crucial, lest the daily grind should warp
    Your better traits by its monotony.
    You've got to blow off steam, lest burn-out spoil   730.
    Your peace of mind, and class become like chain-gang toil.

Ralph Emerson hit the nail on the head:
    You're not a teacher; you're a human being
    Who teaches.   The well-rounded life you've led
    Will buoy you up and keep you bright, while freeing 735.
    You from th' alternative career he gave:
    No more a man, just an extremely well-trained slave.

Along this line, you'll find that language schools
    Divide into two groups: those that attract
    A staff   made up of loafers, duds and fools;   740.
    And those who give the profs leeway to act.

Another day we'll treat administrators,
The helpful allies, and the myopic dictators.

Be a lone wolf, or seek a school where reign
Respect and independence for the ones   745.
Who do the teaching; shun the ones that drain
Your energy and zeal.   The boss who runs
The institute with nagging isn't worth
Killing yourself for, not for all the cash on Earth.

Well, here we are.   It's time for me to knock   750.
'Em dead once more; my students wait within.
Since you're through for the day, why not take stock
Of your untapped potential, so you'll win
The next round.   Ciao for now.   Give me a call
This evening, eightish, if we haven't covered all.   755.

Malleus.   I'll phone you, though I know not to expect
Quick answers to the fix I'm in.

Forceps.   Go see

A movie.   Unwind.   Later on, reflect
On how to build your teaching mastery.

Malleus.　I'll get it nailed down.　Nevermore will I　　　760.
　　Be caught off guard, no matter how my students try.

Forceps.　You're wrong.　The quest for excellence goes on until
　　You turn your toes up.　Challenges appear each day, and
　　always will.

Envoy

Love of potential, love for an ideal
Inspires the gard'ner to brave thorns and heat: 765.
The present's naught, the future is what's real.
He knows at first his love's a one-way street.

He may seem cruel: *he weeds and trims and prunes,*
Gets rid of pretty bugs taken for granted.
Thus wantonly he spends his afternoons   770.
With scant respect for how the patch was planted.

I take no credit for the fruit I see.
My task is homely: *to provide a spot*
Teeming with challenges, distraction-free,
But make the flowers bloom?   *That I do not.*

The magic comes from them; I merely bask
In their achievements that refresh me in my task.

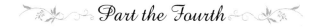
Evening

Prof. Forceps answereth his doorbell.

Forceps.   Madonna!

Malleus.   Though I know you said to phone,
  I took a chance… Oh, dear!   You're not alone.
  Is my face red!   A sylph!   I'd better go.

Forceps.   Come in.   My guest's a nymph you ought to know,
  Since by your posture I deduce you've hit   5.
  Another snag.   I think you'll benefit
  From what she has to say.   She's *Incus* hight.
  Blush not.   We celebrate Minerva's rite,
  Not Cupid's.   Coffee?

Malleus.   Sure.

Incus.   Your visage fey
    And handshake slack catastrophe betray.   10.
    Sit down, kick off your shoes, loosen your tie,
    Take three deep breaths, then tell us what's awry.
    We may assuage your grief; we'll do our best.
    If not, at least you'll get it off your chest.

Forceps.   How do you take it?

Malleus.   Straight.

Incus.   And straight reveal   15.
    The upset that's upset your even keel.
    Shrink not, nor water down, nor prettify
    The horrid turn you've had.   We're standing by.

Malleus.   Consultant!   There's a magic word!   What prof
    Dreams not of casting reason's shackles off,   20.
    And undisturbed by consequences, drone
    Some generalities and cant high-flown,
    Then leave.   For picking up the pieces, those
    Who get the tab for th' emperor's new clothes
    May sort things out, or junk your insights frank,   25.
    As sobbing loud you scramble to the bank.

Incus.   If bosses pay strangers to shoot the breeze
    Rather than listen to their employees,
    Why not make hay?

Forceps.   Agreed.   The fees are fat,
    And slumming now and then reminds you that   30.
    Despite the petty irritations, we
    Monopolize the golden mean: a fee
    For stimulating work.

Incus.   Unless you bow
    To bogus preconceptions that allow
    No freedom, to the laws of crock'ry gods   35.
    That set you and reality at odds.

Forceps.   I never cease to marvel at my friends
    Who wearily attempt to gain their ends
    By systems cursed with built-in boredom.   Down
    The tubes they go, bewitched by the renown   40.
    Of method or man, nor grasp that the fault
    Lies with some hobbyhorse not worth its salt.

Malleus.   Perhaps you'd boil that down.   You've given me
    Class rules; now one for burn-out.

Forceps.   Modesty
      Forbids…

Incus.   Oh, please!

Forceps.   Well, then, if learning's fun,   45.
      And teaching's how this merry task is done,
      If it's not stimulating, you're not teaching,
      But doing something else: or overreaching
      Yourself with theoretic dialog
      (Read: talking to yourself) and in a fog,   50.
      Or baby-sitting.   Which sad sack are you?

Malleus.   None of th' above.   I've come from thumbing through
      Textbooks, in search of one to recommend
      T' a mammoth firm with lots of bucks to spend.

Incus.   You benefited from their habits staid.   55.
      They could have spent some time instead, and made
      Decisions first-hand.

Forceps.   Nay!   They need a scout,
      Lest rascals turn their pockets inside-out.
      We must distinguish 'tween the lazy boss
      Who hires consultants who will bear his cross,   60.

And enterprising chaps who're groping in
Our field, whose life's work elsewhere did begin,
But with expansion need quick expertise.
I'm always honored to help folks like these.
But books, you say?   Alas, the trees that fell   65.
For some I've seen, gimmicky tomes that sell
More by default than merit.

Incus.   Since the night
Is young, let's help our comrade in his plight.
Lead us to where the motley volumes lie;
The garish covers that offend the eye,   70.
The margins vast that frame a puny thought
The corny cartoons, typos that, unsought,
Do impudent bestride the flimsy page,
Plainly the product of scribbler, not sage.

Forceps.   Betake us, then, to where these jury-built   75.
Papyri stained with ink casually spilt
Await our scrutiny, invite our sighs
For the big picture, come, let's grangerize.

In Officina Mallei

Forceps. Phlogiston!   I could smell the stuff a mile Away.

Incus. No wonder you looked pale.   One whiff   80.
 Too many of this makes a chap senile
 Before his time: it's what bad teachers sniff
 Instead of glue, the theoreticians' kif.
 Open the windows!

Forceps. Leave the door ajar!

Malleus. What's going on?   You carry on as if   85.
 The yellow rain that falls when the red star
 Rises, or pestilence were hov'ring where we are.

Forceps. Phlogiston!   Curse of thought since time began!

Incus. Phlogiston!   The flaw-spawning parasite!

Forceps. Phlogiston!   I'll describe it if I can.   90.

Malleus. Describe it, then, but with less heat, more light.

Forceps. The stuff has always been there, but the blight
    Acquired its name when alchemists would try
    To make their calculations come out right
    By adding a fudge factor. Then their eye   95.
    Naught but th' eidolon sought; aloof, they passed facts by.

Incus. They'd managed to find out with methods loose
    Combustion's three components, but they knew
    There's job security in a wild goose
    Chase, so cooked up a fourth out of the blue,   100.
    Guaranteed not t' exist; they could pursue
    Phlogiston, as they called it, full-time. Heat,
    Air, fuel, were too vulgar for gents who
    Either by inclination were effete,
    Or knew that jabberwocky leads to easy street.   105.

Malleus. You say phlogiston, then where others say
    Black box.

Forceps. Eh?

Incus. Run that by again.

Forceps. Black hole?

Malleus.   No, box.   I read about it yesterday.
   An engineer thus decorates his scroll
   For brevity: he gives a module's role   110
   And place, no more elsewhere he gives details.
   The author I perused used it in droll
   Wise: terms employed when scrutinizing fails,
   Where all agree that from no eye will fall the scales.

Incus.   Like instinct.

Malleus.   Right.   People take it at face   115.
   Value, and by convention glibly bandy
   The word about.

Incus.   Professional.

Malleus.   Class.

Incus.   Race.

Forceps.   Centrifugal force, gravity were dandy,
   Much like the stork: lazy minds find them handy
   For making their evasions smooth as silk,   120.
   To quash pert questions, lull keen minds to blandly
   Swallow the palliatives like mothers' milk.

Placebos guard the sinecure granted their ilk.

I'll keep your black box, a repository
   Wherein I'll tuck much mental sleight of hand   125.
   I've seen, new-fangled tricks and chestnuts hoary;
   Having defined it, though, wit's laws demand
   We own the thoughts, though kindred, sep'rate stand.
Incus.   Let's say black box is when all follow suit
   When one cries "shut, sesame," when the sand   130.
   Is noggin-riddled; hot active pursuit
   Of grail or Prester John is all phlogiston's fruit.

Those maddened overnight prolific grow:
   They pound their punch-drunk typewriters amain,
   Amok, their ink-lust waxing with each blow,   135.
   Berserk, they cut a swath with sable stain;
   The front expands as margins start to wane.
   The field is strewn with mangled words that groan
   For Liquid Paper's balm, but moan in vain;
   Their gen'rals live for the attack alone: 140.
   They can't have om'lettes without being error-prone.

Malleus.   But in my office?

Forceps.   It's these books that reek,
    Steeped as they are in quaint quixotic lore.
    You'll understand after we've had a peek,
    See good and bad as over them we pore;   145.
    They can be used, if you know what t' ignore.
    Phlogiston's scent's the giveaway, the tip
    That warns of reefs between you and the shore.
    You'll keep a-moving at a decent clip,
    Nor stranded be by wrack of others' authorship.   150.

The random page test, come!

Incus.   Let's see.   I'll start
    With this one, jacketed in colors chaste
    And with the least offensive cover art.
    You do the honors.

Malleus.   Hmm.   The page is graced
    With photographs aplenty, nicely spaced,   155.
    But unclear.

Forceps.   Read the caption.

Malleus.   "Scorpios…"

Incus.   Oh, please!

Malleus.   I'll skip a bit.   "Granola's taste…"

Forceps.   Keep skipping.

Malleus.   "Watergate…"

Forceps.   It's one of those.
You'll find the Beatles, draft resistance; so it goes.

I call these books time capsules, since they date   160.
The moment   when their authors grew hidebound,
The ones who thought the Sixties were so great,
Their smug world echoing to Neil Young's sound.
They still lose sleep because McGovern wound
Up short; for them the pinnacle of wit   165.
Is Nixon imitations; when they've found
The *Easy Rider*'s back, they have a fit:
Misty with mem'ries, don their beads and write a bit.

Incus.   Let's flip through this one, bold red white and blue.
Malleus.   The eagle rampant, or, betrays its thrust: 170.
There's propaganda beneath that tatoo;
That's why I'd just as soon it gathered dust.

I deal with history, as we all must,
But show the forest, not the cherry tree.
The greatness of this land can't be discussed   175.
Unless you tell the truth unflinchingly,
And show all of the lurid, splendid tapestry.

When asked, I send them trotting off to glean
Crucial specifics, off the beaten track:
Of Garfield, shot because his hands were clean;   180.
Of Douglass, Carver, Joplin and the Black;
Witch hunters, and the ones who beat them back;
The sordid origins of Chinatown;
Of Nisei told they had two hours to pack,
But also how they couldn't be kept down;   185.
And Washington refusing to accept a crown.

You'll see its rival somewhere in the heap,
Its cover like a snapshot spread designed,
As varied as the morgues the papers keep.
More fit a hatchet of the Roman kind,   190.
The emblem of those with an axe to grind.
A litany of wrongs and ills and needs
Can't compensate for lack of meat you find
Between the covers.   Sowing tares but leads
To forests felled to mulch phlogiston-oozing weeds. 195.

Incus.   I don't much mind obtrusive points of view.
    So what if th' author goes out on a limb?
    Look at the nuts and bolts, not the loose screw;
    Just ask for explanations full, yet prim;
    Some readings that are hard, and some to skim;   200.
    Word lists and grammar notes that correspond
    To normal English, not to pedant's whim;
    That's all you need.   If th' author flits beyond
    The basics, it won't hurt t' indulge his fancies fond.

Did I say something wrong?   You winced.   Yes, both.   205.
    Let's have it.

Forceps.   Grammar.

Malleus.   Our trade's fatal flaw.
    Mere mention of it makes me blush, and loath
    To think how oft I've set up rules of straw,
    Crude generalities that pass for law
    To none but English teachers, who ignore   210.
    The rules that they defend with tooth and claw,
    The minute the last student's out the door.
    Phlogistonisms we expound, dare not explore.

Forceps.   How do I envy, spouting shades of gray,

The Punjab pundit's vivid red and black,   215.
And how Swahili, in its meaty way,
Puts people on foundations that won't crack
The Russ, the Turk, the Hebrew have no lack
Of neat mnemonic cues that regiment
Their rambling verbs.   By contrast, I'm a quack: 220.
Dare not defend the system I present;
Osmosis, not me, makes my students eloquent.

Incus.   Haven't you heard?   Confusion is old hat.
I jotted down the reference, and I stuck
It in my purse...hang on... I'll have it stat.   225.
While rummaging, I'll paraphrase.   As luck
Would have it, there's a breakthrough that will tuck
Away loose ends, explain verbs in a trice.
Just think of all the jargon we can shuck!
I haven't heard simpler, neater advice   230.
Since Doctor Panini made patients say "ah" twice.

Malleus.   Keep paraphrasing as you rummage still.
Oft I've suspected verbs could be explained;
I smelled a rat when faced with "shall" and "will."
Though that got squared away, much yet remained.   235.
Dissatisfied, I long to be retrained.
I grasp the trunk and tail; the pachyderm

Eludes me, so I blunder on with strained
Pseudolatinity.   Lead me to firm
Ground where language reality will match the term.   240.

Incus.   You've got it backwards.   Stand back from the puzzle.
Grammar's not *a priori*, so it's best
In Luther's words, to "look folks in the muzzle."
Resemblance to your mother tongue's the test;
Keep learnéd cuckoo's eggs out of your nest.   245.
The mongrel shun: try for a standard breed.
The Romans, mark my words, would be distressed
To know that they're invoked in times of need:
Wild stabs at Varro's style make buried Caesar bleed.

Forceps.   Give archaeology, and give your purse   250.
A rest.   A later dig will yield the note.
Not paper, but a paper tiger's curse
Concerns us, archaisms learned by rote.
But listen, any fool can rock the boat.   255.
Sure, standard jargon stinks; and Queen Anne's dead.
No shell game's needed, but an antidote.
At least our hokum's standardized.   I'll shed
My bunkum quick, but only if truth's in its stead.

Incus.　Remember to forget the prior names
　　　　Of misconceptions I won't dignify　　　　　　260.
　　　　With repetition of their wobbly claims.
　　　　Time marches on, and they deserve to die.
　　　　The *Timeless* form's the one that we apply
　　　　To thoughts whose information counts alone.
　　　　　"Time marches on" itself does not imply　　265.
　　　　A context, so it floats there on its own.
　　　　The verb is plain vanilla, and it's carved in stone.

"What are you doing this weekend?" we say.
　　　　The "be" plus suffix "-ing" I thus explain:
　　　　The form is *Limiting*.　We thus convey　　　270.
　　　　Acts with beginnings, ends, or both.　Restrain
　　　　The urge to make this homely word arcane,
　　　　Especially by giving Father Time
　　　　More than his due.　Limit yourself, maintain
　　　　The nuance you observe.　Recall, your prime　　275.
　　　　Objective's finding facts, most dowdy, few sublime.

Be undeceived by context when you hear
　　　　The *Distant* form, abundant but unsplit.
　　　　"If I went," "Then I went" may first appear
　　　　To need two sep'rate tags to make things fit.　　280.
　　　　Put down your scalpel and reflect a bit:

One's distant from reality; its mate
Shows temp'ral distance.   Stop! The target's hit.
Verbosity's a common teacher's trait.
But learn to shut your mouth, move on, pass up the bait.
                                                                285.
"I have discussed three forms" another shows.
To "have" we join the verb form called the third
(No other name's as clear) and so disclose
Th' experience exists.   I've picked a word
I've heard computerniks use and conferred   290.
It on the *Scanning* form, that verifies
In noncommittal way.   It's vague and blurred,
Tight-lipped and grudging, shunning temp'ral ties;
In practice, oft accompanied by alibis.

The third form, when spiced up with "am" or "be"   295.
        "was, were, become, is are" and slangy "get,"
Conveniently is called *Seventy-three*:
"Be" 's Pleiades are sevenfold; I let
The eighth lurk unaccepted by the set,
Though it may be ennobled in a while.   300.
It's used, it's understood where'er it's met,
Which sentence illustrates its place in style,
As common to mechanic as to bibliophile.

Then mix and match the moods I "was describing."
    That illustrates the crazy quilt in fine: 305.
    It's *Distant Limiting*, which you'd find jibing
    With speech you'd heard before this speech of mine.
    "Had heard" you heard in the preceding line
    Is *Distant Scanning*, and analogous
    Approaches, calmly figured out, untwine   310.
    Any old phrase you might chance to discuss;
    After the dust has settled, "there'll have been" no fuss.

I hope you get the hints I'm getting at,
    And use them to get by, and get around
    Old nomenclature.   You'll get over that.   315,
    Don't let it get you down until you've found
    Ways to get your ideas through safe and sound,
    Not just to get by with getting off.
    Get with the tricks I'm trying to expound
    And you'll get up the courage not to scoff   320.
    When urged to ruminate, not patronize the trough.

That was a bit contrived, but it will serve
    To show that *Two-word Verbs* (and sometimes *Three-*)
    Enrich the tongue's precision and its verve.
    The Viking in our language fam'ly tree   325.
    Demands its due from genealogy.

Word-origins prove nothing, but they aid
The sinking-in, and cut down on drudgery:
Context and content firmly you must braid
Since expositions that are colorful won't fade.   330.

I may have garbled or omitted some,
    But that's the gist of what the authors said.
    Although I don't know where they got it from,
    They've paved the way as far as I could tread;
    Their stepping-stones still beckon me ahead.   335.
    Oh, there's some mopping up to do, since my
    Brief echo of their thought's not gold, but lead.
    The scene is tidied up.   We're free to ply
    Our trade with honor, and look students in the eye.

Forceps   So, free at last!   Analogies had we,   340.
    In one observer's tart satiric view,
    To "Newton's Seven Laws of Gravity:"
    First, "Apples fall on Saturday;" rule two
    Was "Apples fall on Sunday," carried through
    The week.   Now Monday can be grammar day,   345.
    The others for what we're supposed to do:
    Forge skill from concepts, not fritter away
    Our time on rules none are expected to obey.

To teach a chap to tie his shoes, you need
    No time spent on the history of laces;   350.
    The brain can rest, and let the fingers lead.
    Concepts and skills live in diff'rent brain-places:
    Maxims kill class time, but they leave no traces
    On rough and ready areas that guide
    Mouth-muscles, that need putting through their paces
                                  355.
    For kinesthetic reasons.   Set aside
    The Hamletizing cortex, since its hands are tied.

Singers and fencers must deactivate
    Extraneous cerebral regions which
    Distract, intrude or make them hesitate.   360.
    If not, the swordsman's poked; the singer's pitch
    Goes haywire.   Language doubts produce the hitch
    The mars the accent, makes the student blush.
    The higher neuron centers cause the glitch,
    Hobble the vocal chords, turn tongues to mush.   365.
    They make the easy shot veer toward the underbrush.

Since idiots and children learn to speak,
    Infer that mental freight's supremacy
    At worst makes prospects for improvement bleak,
    At best is not all it's cracked up to be.   370.

Part the Fourth: Evening ✳

The coach does all the dirty work.   It's he,
Not the omniscient sportscaster we ought
To imitate.   Though your Master's debris
May soothe you, don't give it a moment's thought,
But watch your students' mouths to gauge how much you've taught.
375.

Malleus.   I understand how Dubliners must feel,
Who knew which side their *beard* was buttered on,
But with *Ulysses* corrected, must deal
With Joyce, not Freudian slips that typos spawn.
Think of th' analyses to be withdrawn!
Once blooming prophets, now over a barrel;
Their darkling mysteries die with the dawn.
As Milton's Yuletide spooks distraught to carol,
So gibber they; the emperor seeks new apparel.

And here I float in zero gravity.   385.
    Satori's like that, I suppose: you swap
    Your heaviness through mental alchemy
    For a handful of air, all at one pop.
    Illumination's wearing, though.   Let's stop
    And take a brain-siesta.   What's been sown   390.
    Needs time to sprout.   Priestess, your manna-drop
    Was most impressive.   I, Oblomov's clone,

Am grateful when an Olga kind throws me a bone.

How came you here?   Whose liv'ry do you wear?
    You're on a leave of absence, I divine;   395.
    Fact-finding, right?   as when with time to spare
    Krishna cavorts with keepers of the kine.
    Where's your home base?   I fain would know the shrine.
    I'd thither trot to gape and be inspired,
    Pay homage to your Sarastro benign.   400.
    Whose crest bear you when not mufti-attired?

Incus.   A glad unmastered ronin I: I just got fired.

Though caught off guard when ordered to make tracks,
    I'd seen a pattern, but I chose to wink:
    Each time our best and brightest got the ax,   405.
    To fill his shoes, they hired a missing link.
    Robots are more abundant than you'd think.
    Peer-dialog began to dwindle, when
    My world and theirs grew daily out of synch.
    That irked me, since yours truly'd always been   410.
    One of the gang; now lion in a Daniel's den.

    But I hung on, hoping the tide would turn.
    Then came the bull; pink paper bore the news.

I saw the time had come for me t' adjourn
Sine die, cleaned out my desk, dusted my shoes,   415.
And left the field to zombies, wimps and shrews.
As when a surfer is tsunami-borne
And has no time to waft shoreward adieus
I fluttered from the drab cocoon I'd worn,
My way confetti-strewn with warning memos torn.   420.

That's how Cordelia made it here to France.

Forceps.   But will you stay?   The homing instinct's strong;
    Routine may yet exert a pull.

Incus.   Fat chance.

Forceps.   Think of your students, though, who did no wrong.

Incus.   Oh, please!

Forceps.   Besides, you won't stay free for long: 425.
    Our racket's organized; where'er you light
    The mediocre ones control the tong.
    It's everywhere.   My counsel is: sit tight.
    Save your God-given ammo; bullets are to bite.
    In my coat pocket... wait... are letters three.   430.

That's odd. They're four. No matter. I had scanned
Them when you came a-calling. Let these be
My evidence that everywhere you land
You'll find no chief withholds his clammy hand.
Since all three…

Malleus. Four.

Forceps. The fourth's for me. The rest   435.
Are sent to "all the gang." They take the stand,
My witnesses that fouled is every nest,
The teacher's held to be a necessary pest.

Prof. Forceps readeth his mail.

Epistle the First

My hand shakes, a persistent headache throbs;
    You guessed it: a new sub-boss came today,   440.
Assuring us we didn't know our jobs,
    That we'd all be fired if he had his way.
(The last one was his clone; he's since moved on:
    The grass is greener on the dung-hill slope)

I listened to his silly threats, took notes   445.
   While stifling a yawn.
He'll go before he does much harm, I hope;
   But drunk with pow'r for now, he sneers and gloats.

The torch is passed, as Samson passed it to
   His vulpine allies: no illumination;   450.
This fresh firebrand portends but havoc new.
   Lo, littler foxes swarm to make oblation:
My comrades once, now jackals seeking favor.
   They jostle, snout to dusky snout, should he
      Throw them a bone, make one his hatchet man.   455.
      Like Pavlov's dogs they slaver,
Eager for a toehold in tyranny:
   They vie to catch his eye as best they can.

Could I, could I but find th' assembly line
   Where mediocrity takes human form,   460.
Then slinks away to harass me and mine,
   I'd try to modify the boorish norm.
A sense of humor, earthy wisdom I'd
   Slip in somehow, in paranoia's place;
      To save on ulcer medicine, they'd find   465.
      Humility instead of pride,
Momentum, not the fear of losing face,

Thinking ahead, no guilty glance behind.

But since that goal is out of reach for now,
  I daydream of upcoming interviews   470.
And flight to schools whose policies allow
   Me room to do my best, where no boss chews
Me out because my quest for quality
   Ignores his dream: an empire populated
    By grov'ling robots, sycophants and spies, 475.
    Where his supremacy
Makes this our school his harem, where, elated,
  All cheer his flops, excuses, alibis.

As I define our trade, it's aeons old;
   Some say it's but a few decades of age,   480.
And try to stop reform and progress cold,
   Freezing the field, praising its present stage.
As once brash hippies shake their graying heads
   At anything before or after rock
    And roll, conformity's the new ideal. 485.
    Our Agamemnon dreads
All save the safe routine, the standard spiel.

I live at peace with visionaries, though
   By temp'rament I seek t' explore the past. 490.

Our ancestors learned lingos long ago
And seem t' have picked them up smoothly and fast.

I aim for their success, and that's enough
For me, but since our object is the same
I love to chat with pioneers, to view   495.
Their bits of airy fluff
And firebird feathers, play the lively game
Of stripping truisms from what is true.

Now, though, the pressure's on: it's not a matter
Of how we teach, but if we teach at all.   500.
Survival's not in class, but how we flatter,
And since I see the writing on the wall
I'll follow my comrades who've left already,
Drop you a line when I've found me a spot
With fairness, trust and frankness that I need   505.
To keep my morale steady:
A place as yet untainted by the rot
That finds me blue, will find me fired or freed.

*   *   *

Epistle the Second

It is a chalk-smudged pedagogue
    Who stops three as they stroll   510
From a successful interview
    That found them on a roll.

"How now, old timer," one exclaims
    This is a clean suit.   Scram!
Lay off your powd'ry hand, forsooth!"   515.
    The elder sighs, "You lamb!

"Lest your John Hancock work you woe,
    Heed me, before you ink
Your declaration of dependence;
    Pause you on the brink."   520.

The other two go gaily on,
    The third, enthralled, must bide:
The oldster's spell has mastered him,
    He hearkens glassy-eyed.

The Tale

Though gaunt and frazzled, know my years   525.
    But five-and-twenty are;
My haggard mien, my stoop are new;
    I once was up to par.

Straight-backed and steely-eyed I strode,
    Name-dropping with the best,   530.
The envy of my colleagues, who
    Would gape at me, impressed.

I knew my craft, from colored chalk
    To fancy 'lectric gear.
Tight-lipped, I'd point to letters pied;   535.
    A pin-drop could you hear.

Calliope, whose strictest law
    Is gladness to the sense,
Invoked I, and students' desire
    Bent toward obedience.   540.

The girls in class would fling themselves

At me to pick and choose,
Hermetic I disdained to stoop,
    Wed to the teaching muse.

My articles found honored nooks   545.
    In thick anthologies,
And editors would waft my words
    To readers overseas.

'Twas but with condescension I
    Would deign to teach at all.   550.
I longed to lead my peers to truth,
    Cure them of thinking small.

Although I stood in line to be
    A grand old man some day,
After a few gray heads died off,   555.
    I sought a quicker way.

A Ganymede without a Jove,
    I reasoned, must remain
A puny creature, lacking clout:
    To lead, you have to train.   560.

So I sought out the chap atop

Our local pyramid,
Requesting an apprenticeship,
To learn the tricks he did.

His blank eyes narrowed, but no twitch   565.
Played on his poker face.
"Yes, we can work together.   How's
Morale around the place?

"To make decisions, one can't go
On instruments, stone blind.   570.
The first step in your o.j.t.'s
The grapevine's pulse to find.

"Report to me the things you hear
And I'll evaluate
Retentive skills, ear for details,   575.
The zeal you demonstrate."

I lay choice rumors at his feet,
And felt a partner's joy
At seeing colleagues told to go
Elsewhere to seek employ.   580.

A certain coldness did I sense,

But I was too self-centered
To take note of the pause that fell
    On rooms in which I entered.

Then came the fatal day when I   585.
    Incurred my mentor's wrath.
I'd relayed a red herring dropped
    In cold blood in my path.

"You made me look ridiculous,"
    He howled; his breast he smote.   590.
"Your days as an informant are
    Kaput!   That's all she wrote!"

Then kicked upstairs was I, to serve
    The pleasure of my liege.
Though hated, I was always kind;   595.
    You know, noblesse oblige.

A higher caste was I than they,
    A face card in the deck,
And as a badge of honor wore
    The herring 'round my neck.   600.

I spent a year in solitude,

Save for my Master wise.
'Twas first-rate training in the arts
Of threats, evasions, lies.

My Master got a better job,   605.
And spat me out among
The little people I despised,
Down on the bottom rung.

The word was out.   Pariah now
I wander, outcast, blest   610.
But with this herring skeleton
That dangles on my chest.

The next guy had no use, you see,
For henchmen second-hand.
He chose another, greener one,   615.
Whose training he'd command.

Now you, young cocky applicant,
Bethink you, ere you sign
A year of your short life away;
Recall this fate of mine!   620.

Our status quo here guarantees

You'll either pestered be
Or used, then dumped at pleasure of
 An ingrate Ph. D.

The applicant shakes off his spell;   625.
  The derelict is gone.
Enlightened, he resolves to find
  Some other job anon.

*   *   *

Epistle the Third

I

Awake! No Yawn yet linger on the lips!
As Bailey's Beads proclaim, past's the Eclipse.   630.
Staff meeting's over; time to stretch your legs
And feel the Numbness flee the fingertips.

II

As roses buried 'neath Isfahan's snow,

We come to life again and start to grow.
Though smothered in the Trivial and Trite   635.
We pick up where we were two hours ago.

III

The Ribbon of life's Typewriter has traced
Naught of importance as it forward raced:
The meeting's wisdom boiled down to a note,
One page, one word per line, quadruple spaced!   640.

IV

What matters it, think we, as we break camp,
How oft Aladdin rub the battered lamp
If his emerging Genie but extend
To solve his problems, just a Rubber Stamp?

V

Like Attar's birds, dejectedly we go   645.
To teachers' parliament, our fate to know.
We look into the Glass and it foretells
Sev'n years bad luck, whether broken or no.

VI

Long since the ecstasy has left the Vine,
And Dregs are what we're offered 'stead of wine.　　650.
But lately meetings whet the appetite
More like the wind that's fraught with turpentine.

VII

Plant ye upon my tomb when I am dead
A Grapevine mulched by memos never read,
That by the Scuttlebutt that it conveys　　　　655.
My colleagues know what's Up, despite what's Said.

VIII

When the Grand Eunuch grabs you by the hair
Before your flying carpet mounts the air,
Turn up the nearer corner by the fringe!
Show him you know what's been swept under there. 660.

IX

A spider saved the Prophet, so they say,
By spinning camouflage o'er where he lay.
When comes th' Inquisitor, hold you not back;
A little Fudging goes a long, long way.

X

When the Chief Dervish lets none disagree,   665.
As Ali Baba's cave oped to no key
Save to a secret password, strive to find
The jargon-addict's "open sesame."

XI

Oases in the desert vanish clean:
The caravan finds dust where they were seen.   670.
The First may fool you, but the next Mirage
From grand Solutions should the trav'ler wean.

XII

Should you before some smitten Blackboard stand,
Recall: others taught here, and they got canned.
Erase their Scribblings gently, since your Turn   675.
Will come in time, for so is the world planned.

XIII

But now, dear pilgrim, get you off to class;

Take comfort in instructing lad and lass.

In good times and in bad, repeat you low,

Or write it on the wall: This too shall pass!   680.

*   *   *

I rest my case.

Incus.   Oh, pooh!

Forceps.   And here I stand.

Excuse me while I check this little note,

The fourth one, while I have it in my hand.

Let's pause for you to ponder, me to gloat.

Incus.   You lose, precisely 'cause of what they wrote...   695.

Malleus.   What's wrong?   You haven't even heard her yet.

Incus.   Not me, you goose.   The envelope, I'll bet,

Contains the answer.   Wait.   He'll tell us when he's set.

Forceps.   I'm fired.   Just like that.   They want my key, 700.

And want me gone two weeks from yesterday.

It says I am deficient in *esprit.*

Incus.   Then sit you down.   Hear what I have to say.
This was our topic ere you came our way,
So join your friend, be seated.   Both, recall   705.
Epistles one through three, their tenor gray;
Fix in your minds the pit, avoid the fall.
Hang tough, and I'll explain how we can have it all.

Your correspondents give an overview
Precise, consistent, crisp.   But look beyond;   710.
Th' aquarium is not the ocean blue.
The lake awaits, and then the sea.   The pond
Won't change or overflow to correspond
To metamorphoses or growth you show;
Nor feel a void when you choose to abscond.   715.
It incubates the egg, feeds embryo,
But at maturity, it's time for you to go.

Nature has ways to let you know the score:
Keep hanging 'round, and all you get is flak;
Red carpet, but rolled out at the back door;   720.
A nudge, a push, and then a lusty smack.
You walk on water, but when things are slack
You're jettisoned.   When squalls arise, the mast
Is cut away, heaved over at one whack.
Ballast personified fights to the last: 725.

The clods queue up to see by whom the first stone's cast.

So what about it?　Let's all make the jump.
　　There's feudalism here, so what's to lose?
　　Let's strike out on our own and leave this dump;
　　We've been around the block, and paid our dues.　　730.
　　Clients are out there; the question is:　whose?
　　I say, hang up a shingle, shake the tree,
　　Make 'em an offer that they can't refuse.
　　If Wal-Mart did it, by George, so can we;
　　With elbow grease, free enterprise will set us free.　735.

Malleus.　Banzai!　I quit, effective here and now.
　　I'll get these books and finish them at home

Incus.　And you?

Forceps.　I'm ready, coach.　I'll trust the Tao.

Malleus.　On second thought, no need for me to comb
　　Through flimsy pamphlet and pretentious tome.　　740.
　　Now I begin to twig, and see the thread.
　　In all these books, all roads lead one to roam,
　　But on a leash:　the damage doesn't spread.
　　The teacher's wings are clipped; the books flutter instead.

Forceps. That stands to reason. Good help's hard to find. 745.

Malleus. These volumes, then, are safety nets that shield
The student, lest his mind be undermined
By neophytes who want to sweep the field.
The learner, at least has a book to wield;
It's better safe than sorry. Compromise 750.
Dictates they choose secure, though middling yield,
And hence the paper blinkers on their eyes;
The rhadamanthine rules at least homogenize.

Forceps. There's more to talk about, but it will keep.

Incus. It's past my bedtime, boys. Let's call it quits. 755.

Malleus. I'm not up to another quantum leap;
Let's part for now, rejoin when time permits.

Incus. I'll check my schedule book and see what fits.
It's in my purse... oh, where?... Voici. I guess
Tomorrow... Say! Here are those grammar wits, 760.
The two I earlier quoted, more or less:
Phoenix and Lindeman cleaned up the mess.

Forceps. I'll look them up mañana. Now, though, let's recess.

Envoy

The House of Mirrors at the county fair!
I've wondered (th' implications are sublime)   765.
If sometime people don't get trapped in there
And led out by the hand at closing time.

Too much reflection leaves you standing still
And living in a glass house, as it were.
Though like Narcissus you may gape your fill,   770.
You'll miss the fun outside, unless you stir.

Dead ends and detours teach us; comfort numbs.
Escape, later sort out the lessons hard.
Shameful to wait till to your rescue comes
A chuckling carny playing Saint Bernard.   775.

I've been enriched by being lost and found.
I choose the sky; I've spent time underground.

Finis

語言文學類　PG0266

Hammer & Tongs
Conversations in Verse Concerning English Teaching

作　　者 / Michael Skupin
發 行 人 / 宋政坤
執行編輯 / 詹靚秋
圖文排版 / 鄭維心
封面設計 / 蕭玉蘋
數位轉譯 / 徐真玉　沈裕閔
圖書銷售 / 林怡君
法律顧問 / 毛國樑　律師
出版印製 / 秀威資訊科技股份有限公司
　　　　　臺北市內湖區瑞光路 583 巷 25 號 1 樓
　　　　　電話：02-2657-9211　　　傳真：02-2657-9106
　　　　　E-mail：service@showwe.com.tw
經 銷 商 / 紅螞蟻圖書有限公司
　　　　　臺北市內湖區舊宗路二段 121 巷 28、32 號 4 樓
　　　　　電話：02-2795-3656　　　傳真：02-2795-4100
　　　　　http://www.e-redant.com

2009 年 6 月 BOD 一版
定價：200 元

讀　者　回　函　卡

感謝您購買本書，為提升服務品質，煩請填寫以下問卷，收到您的寶貴意見後，我們會仔細收藏記錄並回贈紀念品，謝謝！

1. 您購買的書名：＿＿＿＿＿＿＿＿＿＿＿＿＿＿＿＿＿＿＿

2. 您從何得知本書的消息？

　　□網路書店　□部落格　□資料庫搜尋　□書訊　□電子報　□書店

　　□平面媒體　□ 朋友推薦　□網站推薦　□其他＿＿＿＿＿＿

3. 您對本書的評價：(請填代號　1.非常滿意 2.滿意 3.尚可 4.再改進)

　　封面設計＿＿＿　版面編排＿＿＿　內容＿＿＿　文/譯筆＿＿＿　價格＿＿＿

4. 讀完書後您覺得：

　　□很有收穫　□有收穫　□收穫不多　□沒收穫

5. 您會推薦本書給朋友嗎？

　　□會　　□不會，為什麼？＿＿＿＿＿＿＿＿＿＿＿＿＿＿＿＿＿＿

6. 其他寶貴的意見：＿＿＿＿＿＿＿＿＿＿＿＿＿＿＿＿＿＿＿＿＿

＿＿＿＿＿＿＿＿＿＿＿＿＿＿＿＿＿＿＿＿＿＿＿＿＿＿＿＿＿＿＿

＿＿＿＿＿＿＿＿＿＿＿＿＿＿＿＿＿＿＿＿＿＿＿＿＿＿＿＿＿＿＿

＿＿＿＿＿＿＿＿＿＿＿＿＿＿＿＿＿＿＿＿＿＿＿＿＿＿＿＿＿＿＿

讀者基本資料

姓名：＿＿＿＿＿＿＿＿＿＿　年齡：＿＿＿＿　性別：□女　□男

聯絡電話：＿＿＿＿＿＿＿＿　E-mail：＿＿＿＿＿＿＿＿＿＿＿

地址：＿＿＿＿＿＿＿＿＿＿＿＿＿＿＿＿＿＿＿＿＿＿＿＿＿＿＿

學歷：□高中(含)以下　　□高中　　□專科學校　　□大學

　　　□研究所(含)以上　□其他＿＿＿＿＿＿＿＿

職業：□製造業 □金融業 □資訊業 □軍警 □傳播業 □自由業

　　　□服務業 □公務員 □教職　 □學生 □其他＿＿＿＿＿＿

To：114

台北市內湖區瑞光路 583 巷 25 號 1 樓

秀威資訊科技股份有限公司　　收

寄件人姓名：

寄件人地址：□□□

(請沿線對摺寄回,謝謝!)

秀威與 BOD

BOD（Books On Demand）是數位出版的大趨勢，秀威資訊率先運用 POD 數位印刷設備來生產書籍，並提供作者全程數位出版服務，致使書籍產銷零庫存，知識傳承不絕版，目前已開闢以下書系：

一、BOD 學術著作—專業論述的閱讀延伸
二、BOD 個人著作—分享生命的心路歷程
三、BOD 旅遊著作—個人深度旅遊文學創作
四、BOD 大陸學者—大陸專業學者學術出版
五、POD 獨家經銷—數位產製的代發行書籍

BOD 秀威網路書店：www.showwe.com.tw
政府出版品網路書店：www.govbooks.com.tw

永不絕版的故事・自己寫・永不休止的音符・自己唱